DESCENDANTS
OF ROBIN HOOD

Guardian

OF THE

North

MAGGIE K. WEST

Library of Congress Control Number: 2023906160

978-1-7349447-5-4 (hardcover); 978-1-7349447-3-0 (paperback); 978-1-7349447-4-7 (ebook)

First Jasmine Codex printing, June 2023

13 12 11 10 9 8 7 6 5 4

This book contains subject matter such as moderate violence. For a full list of content warnings, visit www.maggiekwest.com/warnings

Hi Momma and Daddy!

I love you!

Pronunciation Guide

Áccyn (ACK-in)

Ajax (AY-jaah-ks)

Azomien (AH-zoh-mean)

Androuet (AN-droo-et)

Calmier (CAL-meer)

Cloudia (cl-OW-dee-uh)

Daetho (DAY-thoh)

Ealdra (EEL-druh)

Fortunati (fohr-too-NAH-tee)

Gisborne (GIHS-bohrn)

Iversen (EYE-ver-son)

Karalie (kay-ruh-LEE)

Khadija (kuh-DEE-jhuh)

Marcrombie (mar-CRAWM-bee)

Natanian – (nuh-TAN-ee-an)

Niskian (NIGH-skee-en)

Rangerian (rayn-JER-ee-an)

Rehynall (REH-nahll)

Rowan (ROW-inn)

Tyrest (TEYE-rehst)

PROLOGUE

A COLD BREEZE RUSTLED through the forest branches. Huddled around a campfire in the darkness, a band of men drank, their long swords resting on the ground. The men's shadows seemed to leap from the fire to flicker against the trees. Several squirrels roasted over the flames.

"Hey, Orin!" a tall, scruffy man shouted, swinging his wooden tankard. The skinny, teenage boy he was speaking to simply ran a sharpening stone across his sword, saying nothing.

"Leave the kid alone, Sheriff," another man chided, leaning back against a tree. He took a swig from his tankard and wiped his beard on his sleeve.

The Sheriff staggered to his feet, drunk on ale. "Hey, Orin!" he called again. "Why don't you pick up that lit'le ole blade there and show me what you got!"

The other man rolled his eyes and turned away as low laughs ran through the camp.

"Come on, *boy!*" The Sheriff seized his long sword and drew it out, splashing his ale across the campfire. The liquid hissed, sending up tendrils of steam. Orin looked up, and his eyes—one blue and one brown—flamed in anger.

"I'm not a boy," he growled.

"Androuet, let him be," the other man tried again, setting down his tankard.

"No." Orin rose to his feet and dropped his sharpening stone. The dark, Damascus of his sword shone in the firelight as though made of molten steel. He took a step forward, to the shouts of the surrounding men.

Sheriff Androuet laughed drunkenly. "That's it, lit'le boy! Come on!"

Orin clenched his fists. The cold breeze around them suddenly turned hot and whipped up, tearing at the branches above, churning the fire into a swirling inferno.

"Is that all?" Sheriff Androuet shouted across the roaring flames. "Do you miss your mummy?" he taunted. "Do you want to go home to your mummy, Orin?"

Orin clenched his teeth, the flames reflected in his mismatched eyes. He raised his sword, and the hot Wind whipped up faster. The trees around him groaned beneath the gale.

"Ohh, back up, boys!" Sheriff Androuet smirked at the boy across the roaring fire and threw his tankard to the ground.

With a shout, Orin sprang forward. The flames parted, and he leaped over the roasting squirrels, swinging his weapon in a wide arc. Androuet sidestepped and caught the blade, throwing his weight against it. The flames roared up behind him. Orin spun and pointed his free hand at Androuet's chest. A blast of hot Wind slammed into the man, tossing him on his back. Orin stepped forward, breathing hard, and raised his sword again, anger flaring in his eyes.

Then a cry rang through the air, and three men emerged from the trees, dragging a fourth—an Áccyn nobleman.

"Oh, ho, what is this?" The Sheriff staggered to his feet.

Orin took a step back into the shadows. His Wind died down around them, the fire returning to a warm crackle. The roasting squirrels were scorched black.

The approaching men halted before Sheriff Androuet and shoved the nobleman to his knees. His mottled green tunic was torn and covered in dirt and specks of blood.

"Who are you?" Androuet shouted, much louder than necessary.

"Tobias Williams," the nobleman said quietly, his voice scratchy and dry. One of the men shoved him, so he fell forward on his hands, bound together. "I know where he is," Lord Williams muttered.

Androuet drew close, eyebrows raised, and bent down, planting his hands on either side of the lord's face. "Where *who* is?"

Lord Williams swallowed. "The fourth Wind, sir."

Orin took a step forward, dropping his arms. *The fourth Wind...* This was it.

"Where?" Androuet demanded.

The lord did not answer. One of the men raised his sword. "Fort Calmier," he whispered quickly.

Only a day's ride from here, no less. Excitement twisted in Orin's chest.

A wide grin spread across Androuet's face as he stood up. He swung his sword and drove it forward. Lord Williams collapsed at his feet.

"Did you hear that, Orin?" He turned around to face the young man, wiping the blood off his sword, his eyes alight with the fire of the hunt. "The North Wind is revealed."

Orin smiled in glee, despite his fury toward Androuet. *East Wind—the Ealdra Princess—was securely hidden away. And the third...* He glanced sideways at another young soldier in a mottled green tunic who was tied to a tree at the edge of the clearing. The boy's mismatched, angry eyes watched them over his gag. The faint whispers of his West Wind power drifted around Orin, raised by the soldier's fear.

"Come on, boys!" The Sheriff shouted to the rest of his band of men, raising his red-stained sword, "The last one's ours!"

ONE

I PUSHED MYSELF OFF the ground, wiping a streak of blood from my stinging mouth, grunting at the pain. Nick advanced.

I spun my sword in my hand and stepped back, bracing myself. Nick lunged forward. I swung my blade up, knocking his weapon away. I spun, and our swords clashed. His flew from his hand and landed in the dirt. He took a step back.

I grinned. "Ha! Third time's the charm."

He smirked, then slammed his hands together, and Lightning arced up his arms, flashing in his mismatched eyes. I dove aside as a bolt of Lightning shot from his outstretched hands. It hit the dirt with a resounding *boom!*

"That's cheating!" I shouted, rolling to my feet. "*Use swords,* Nicolas!"

"Well, you aren't fighting a regular soldier, *Jackson.*"

A blond boy leaning against the fence shouted from the sidelines, "You dropped your sword, Jack. You're dead!"

I cut him a look. "You can shut up." He grinned back.

Nick straightened his leather jacket, picked up my sword and offered it to me. I glanced at the blade, making sure there wasn't any of Nick's Lightning sparking up to the hilt. I grabbed it and leaned back, bracing myself for a sudden attack. Lightning arced up his blade, and he flashed a smirk.

"You can shut up too," I snapped, and lunged.

His blade caught mine in a shower of sparks. He ducked and slashed. I deflected the blow. Tingles of electricity shot up my arms, making me lose hold of my weapon again. I tripped and landed flat on my back. The air rushed out of my lungs.

"Wow, such grace," a voice said. "He's doing great, isn't he, Natanian?" Through my suddenly blurred vision, I saw a girl step up to the fence and prop one foot up on a rail, leaning forward to watch.

The blond boy beside her responded, "It makes you wonder how he'll handle his power." She snorted a laugh, tossing her sandy brown braids.

Nick laughed, moving toward me. I rolled over, gasping for breath.

"Awesome," I muttered. "I have a whole audience." I coughed.

Nick's blade suddenly came down. I kicked out, hitting his leg. He staggered back, limping a step on his bended knee. I snatched my sword out of the dirt and slammed into him with a shout, throwing him to the ground. His blade flew from his hand. I leveled mine for his throat, planting my foot on his chest.

He raised his hands in surrender. "Not bad." Thin lines of electricity curled around his fingers. He grinned.

"Don't—" I warned. He clapped his hands around my shin and I cried out, falling back. "You..." I cursed. Natanian and the girl laughed. Nick pushed himself to his feet, brushed off his leather jacket, and held out his hand.

"I don't trust you." I shook my head and groaned, painfully pushing myself to my feet. "Just wait until I get my power."

"I hate to break it to you." The girl shrugged. "But I don't know how much North Wind is going to do against Nick's Lightning. No matter how strong it'll be, he's still going to kick your butt."

"First, you can shut up too, Kara." I pointed my sword at her. "Second, that's right." I swung the blade back at Nick. "You wait until tonight. I'm going to kick your butt."

"That's not..." Karalie trailed off with a sigh.

I staggered a bit and propped myself against the fence next to Natanian, who was grinning in amusement.

A man stepped out of the archway into the courtyard. "Jackson?" It was Ajax, Captain of the Guard. His face was dark, his forehead creased in worry as he nervously tugged on his dark green suit.

I sheathed my sword, still holding tight to the fence. "What is it?"

Nick's Master, Bancroft, stepped up beside him. His graying hair was pulled back in a ponytail, his arms folded over his chest.

Captain Ajax straightened his sword belt. "King Rehynall requests your presence."

"*Me?*" I glanced at Nick, whispering, "This isn't another one of your secret plotting meetings, is it?"

Nick shook his head.

"And Nicolas," Captain Ajax added.

"Uh-oh," I muttered.

"Immediately," he insisted.

I glanced at Kara and Nick. "Pushy much?" I laughed under my breath.

"*Jackson,*" Master Bancroft chided.

Kara waved me forward. I swallowed nervously and tried a step. My right leg gave out under me. I grabbed hold of the fence post to keep from tumbling into the dirt.

"What happened to you?" Captain Ajax asked.

I pulled myself up with a grunt and slid between the rails, getting my balance. "He did," I answered shortly, nodding at Nick.

Bancroft smacked a gloved hand into the boy's head.

"Hey!" Nick flinched and rubbed his head.

"I thought we discussed not using your power on your friends, Nicolas."

"Yes, Master." He scowled and folded his hands behind his back.

"Have fun, Your Royal Highnesses!" Natanian piped up, sweeping an arm in a mock bow.

"Don't plot any secret missions without me," Kara added.

Nick and I followed Master Bancroft and Captain Ajax out of the courtyard. I glanced back over my shoulder, butterflies swarming in my stomach. Natanian had turned away, but Kara gave a wave, standing with her hand on her sword hilt, watching us go, her clear, mismatched eyes bright in the sunlight.

"Quickly, Jackson," Captain Ajax whispered urgently. "We need your focus."

He led the way down a long, stone corridor toward a heavy, oak door at the end that marked the entrance to the throne room. I had often passed this door, sneaking as close as I could without the guards shooing me away.

"But, what—?"

The Captain cut me off. "Not here."

I swallowed. This time when I approached, the guards gave a short bow and stepped aside. I was crossing into forbidden territory.

Two

K ING REHYNALL AND HIS advisors stood up from the oblong table before me. The king's crown glinted in the sunlight streaming through the window behind him. Captain Ajax took his place at the table.

"I'll be waiting outside," Bancroft whispered. Nick gave a short bow to his Master, and the door swung closed behind us with an echoing *bang*, that make my heart skip into my throat. I dropped into a quick, low bow.

"Take your seat," King Rehynall ordered.

I swallowed, "Yes, Your Royalness." Nick nudged me. I straightened up and followed him around the table to a pair of empty seats across from Captain Ajax, who pulled his own chair in and smoothed his green suit, leaning forward.

"They aren't going to eat you," Nick whispered with a grin.

I laughed nervously, pulled out a chair, and sat down hard—a little too hard. Half-grimacing, I leaned forward and folded my hands on the table, just like Captain Ajax was doing. Nick sat next to me and nervously spun his dark titanium ring around and around his finger, the thin, jagged stripe of silver flashing in the torchlight with every round.

King Rehynall spoke, "Jackson."

I jumped in my seat, rubbing the crick out of my neck. I tried to slap my smile back on my face, but failed.

A brief look of amusement flashed across King Rehynall's face before his serious expression returned. "There is no need to be nervous around us."

"Yes, Your Majesticity."

"'King' is fine, Jackson."

"Right." I cleared my throat. I was gripping my seat so tightly that my knuckles were getting white. I let go, trying to relax.

"Down to business," Captain Ajax said. He sat back, glancing at me.

"Of course," King Rehynall replied, the light shining off the shards of emerald in his crown. Then he addressed me. "Tonight is your Manifestation, Jackson."

"Oh, I know," I blurted out. "You don't need to tell me. It *is* mine." I took a deep breath. *Talk slower, Jack,* I scolded myself.

"Dillon did not come back."

My stomach dropped. I sat back, clenching my hands in my lap.

"That makes two Wind Rangerians who have gone missing in the last three months," Captain Ajax said, glancing at me.

"Not counting the Ealdra princess," King Rehynall added.

"For all we know, she could be behind this."

"That means..." I swallowed. "I'm the fourth." I looked around the table. The butterflies in my stomach suddenly turned cold. "Are you going to tell me what happened to them?"

"We aren't sure." Captain Ajax looked up. "We're suspecting the Sheriff and his Hunters, but we do know Orin Iversen was part of it. And he's Ealdra. Which makes us suspect they may be behind it."

Nick stopped spinning his ring and looked up at the king, daring him to challenge his heritage. I edged away from him as the electric energy began building around him, the way it always did when this subject came up around the castle.

King Rehynall looked right at him. "The Ealdra attacked our palace in Scotland."

My head whipped around. It felt like someone had just slugged me in the stomach. "But I thought the feud between us was dying down," I muttered. "My Grandpa Tyler—"

"So we thought," King Rehynall agreed. "Years of silence. And now this." His eyes fell on Nick. All the advisors were leaning forward, watching my best friend carefully.

Nick spread his fingers on the table and stated very calmly, "I don't know of anything the Ealdra could be planning, or of anything they might be looking for."

"But you are—" the Captain Ajax started.

I widened my eyes at him, trying to get him to *shut up*. Too late.

Nick shot to his feet. *"I know what I am!"* he shouted. "How many times do we have to go through this? Do you doubt my allegiance?"

Thunder rumbled through the throne room. King Rehynall stood up.

"Hey, Nick, chill out," I whispered.

He sat down hard beside me.

"We do not doubt you, Nicolas," the king said slowly, his voice strong. "But you must understand the position we're in." He exchanged glances with Captain Ajax and sat down. "With Jackson's power about to manifest, the last thing we need is for the Sheriff to find out where he is."

Captain Ajax leaned forward, "We have reason to believe there may be a spy already in our court. If there is, we can expect the Ealdra here tonight. Please, Nicolas, will you look around? See if you can tell who might—"

"I *was* Ealdra," Nick interrupted, his Lightning flashing behind his eyes. "That doesn't mean I knew every single Ealdra soldier! If he even exists, I'm not going to be able to find your spy."

"I'm sorry to bring this up, Nicolas," King Rehynall said. "But you are the closest person we have to the inner workings of the Ealdra. You are our best chance to shut down whatever this is before it develops."

A feeling of foreboding crawled through my stomach. Nick sat motionless beside me, his head bowed over his hands, the air buzzing with electricity around him.

"We know they've found something," the king continued. "Something so strong they have decided to turn on us." The king looked back at Nick. "Please, are you sure you don't know of anything? Not even a rumor or a fairytale of this weapon?"

Nick didn't look up. "No. I've got nothing."

I swallowed, the crawling in my stomach inching its way up to my throat. "So... this means they're coming for me, right? Because I'm the last Wind."

"We do not know that for sure." King Rehynall leaned back. "We only know they are hunting Wind Rangerians, and your North Wind is about to manifest tonight. But we will not back down, we will not give in to fear. The ceremony will go on as planned."

Captain Ajax stood up. "We're throwing up extra defenses. Aerial lookouts will be watching the courtyard and outer wall. We're sending out scouts to mark a perimeter. It will be fine."

"Yeah." I swallowed again. "It'll be just great."

THREE

"WHAT ARE YOU DOING up here?" Kara looked around. Her dark skin glowed in the torchlight. "Aren't you supposed to be off guard duty?"

I looked down at my uniform, cleaned and ironed for my Manifestation ceremony. My sword belt was strapped around my waist, the leather newly polished. "Needed to clear my head." I took a deep breath, the crisp, cool air rushing down my lungs, chilling my throat.

"Yeah, sure." Kara raised her hand, and the torch beside her flared up, hot and bright. "Come and warm up." She leaned against the wall.

I shifted closer to the torch and held my hands to the warm flame. I looked out at the night sky over the Missouri forest. The faint lights of St. Louis glinted far away, blurring the stars on the horizon. Flying shapes passed in the darkness—the aerial scouts Captain Ajax had spoken of. The ever-present fog around the castle drifted in the breeze.

My great-grandfather Rowan Tyler brought me up here all the time when I was little, before I had begun training... before he died. I breathed out and leaned against the stone. It was good to be up here with Kara in the few minutes before the ceremony. I'd known her for years, grown up with her here.

The moon passed behind a small cloud. One of only a few in the sky. I could count every star tonight.

"There it is!" Kara pointed up at a cluster of stars high above the trees. I smiled. Sagittarius... Grandpa Tyler said *that* constellation belonged to me, that the Northern power was infused deep inside me, growing by the hour, until one day it would burst free, twisting around my control. *Watch the stars,* he always said. *Every third night after the full moon, watch it pass through the Great Archer. One night, you will stand in the stone courtyard of Fort Calmier, and the whole world will know of Jackson Marcrombie, the Great Guardian of the North.*

I shifted my feet to keep the blood flowing and tugged my mottled green tunic a little tighter around me.

"Nervous?" Kara asked, turning to look at me.

I swallowed and smiled. "Yeah. My grandpa always talked to me about this day. The *one day* is here."

"He was Rangerian of the North Wind too, right?" I nodded. This was it. Almost five months to the day since my fourteenth birthday. Tonight was my Manifestation. Tonight the power of the North Wind would emerge.

"Hey, Jack," came a familiar voice.

I looked around. My mom stood at the top of the battlement stairs.

"It's time, dear."

Kara grabbed my hand, her skin warm to the touch, as it always was with the Fire burning inside her. "You're gonna do great." Her clear eyes shone. Her hand grew hotter and hotter until I gasped, jerking away. She pressed her palm into the cool stone. "Sorry. Still not that great at controlling it."

"We're in it together." I grinned, rubbing my mildly-burnt palm on my tunic.

I followed my mom down the stairs and under the archway that separated the ceremonial courtyard from the training courtyard. Captain Ajax was waiting at the edge. I followed him and my mom around the crowd, stopping at the far end. My dad was waiting there for me. I saw Nick and Natanian sidle into the crowd with their Masters. Kara was watching from her guard post atop the battlements.

A breeze carried the smell of pine through the air. The torches on the battlements and across the courtyard flickered in the wind. Again, I glanced up at the stars. The moon, three days past its full phase, was just beginning to enter Sagittarius, and I was starting to feel very light-headed. Maybe it was nerves, maybe it was the Manifestation beginning. But I was not going to throw up all over the courtiers, like Grandpa Tyler did.

I wished he were here. He had gone through this. He would know just what to say right about now. Or at least offer some smart-aleck joke.

King Rehynall mounted the platform at the front of the crowd. I tugged nervously on my tunic, excitement beginning to grow. *It was time.* My parents nodded encouragement, and I stepped forward.

The crowd, chatting and laughing as they waited, died down to silence. I glanced over my shoulder. Nick stood beside his Master. Natanian gave me a thumbs-up from a few rows away. My head spun. I flashed him a grin that felt more like a grimace, as my insides twisted in nausea.

King Rehynall held out his hand and I mounted the steps, leaving my parents and Captain Ajax at the foot of the platform. Beside the king stood a young man dressed in leather armor, his blond hair smoothed back. He was youngish, in his early thirties. Most of the Masters were older. They had to have been around the block enough times. They had to have trained many Rangerians before, to be assigned a True Born like me. *So what was so special about this man?*

I met my new Master's eyes. He nodded reassuringly. I heard my grandpa's voice in my head: *One day, Jack. One day you will be the next Great Guardian of the North.* Well, that day was here. And I was feeling less like the Great Guardian and more like a week-old hamburger.

Three soldiers soared overhead on their Perytons. The tips of the deers' antlers shone in the moonlight, the feathers rippling across their wings. Guards in their mottled green uniforms lined the battlements, armed with spears or longbows.

I suddenly felt like I had been punched in the stomach. I doubled over with a gasp. King Rehynall was saying something, but I couldn't understand him through the sound of a million ringing bells going off in my head. *Don't pass out, Jack, don't pass out.* I gulped in deep breaths of cold air.

Plastering a smile on my face, I forced myself to straighten up and tried to hear what the king was saying. His voice seemed to come in and out of range. Luckily, I had seen tons of these Manifestation ceremonies in my entire fourteen years, so I knew what he was supposed to be saying. I tried to focus on the words, tried to take my mind off the piercing pain that now stabbed my brain.

"Eight hundred years ago, the Sorcerer Guy of Gisborne from Prince John's court, planted a trap in a last attempt to capture Robin Hood..." *Yeah, yeah; I knew this story. Get on with it.* My brain felt like it had been left on to broil. "...but the curse laid on the Golden Arrow backfired, releasing a burst of pure magic energy into the outlaw." *Only a couple more minutes. Don't pass out, Jack.*

I glanced up at the sky. The moon was almost centered in Sagittarius. The king droned on, "...and as the generations passed, this power weakened more and more, splitting among Robin Hood's descendants to manifest in the form of elemental powers. The eleven strongest among these Rangerians are known as True Borns, born with the pure elements split from the Earth, the Sky, and the Sea."

I could feel ice-cold Wind against my skin beginning to swirl faster and faster, and felt a thrill of excitement, despite the fact that my innards were basically being dry-frozen. *I had waited my whole life for this one night!* I had played it out in my head over and over, hoping I wouldn't pass out or throw up when it finally came. I watched every phase of the moon pass through Sagittarius, imagining how it would look tonight. That one day was here.

Any sensation of sickness and pain vanished. I breathed a sigh of relief and straightened up. Icy Wind was whipping around me in a vortex, tugging at my uniform, ruffling through my hair. I held out my hands, watching the gray mist swirl up my arms. My heartbeat spiked, and I felt the Wind swirl even faster.

"Jackson Marcrombie, True Born Rangerian of the North Wind!" King Rehynall presented, stepping aside. "Jackson, your Master, Kane."

The young, blond man stepped forward and winked. "How do you feel?"

"Not sick!" I grinned, the butterflies hurtling through my gut at Mach 10 in a new rush of excitement.

My mom stepped up to the platform and held out Grandpa's long chain, with gray mist swirling in the silver vial at the end of it. It twisted up into a miniature tornado as it neared me. Kane took the chain, and I bowed my head. He slid it over my neck. Immediately, the Wind died to a gentle breeze. He held out his hand and I grasped his forearm tight, looking up into his eyes.

"I swear to stand by you," his voice rang out over the crowd. He was younger than I'd thought... in his twenties, I would guess, now that I saw him up close.

"To defend you, to train you by sword and power until you are Master." He didn't even blink, his bright blue eyes a bit unnerving.

I swallowed and recited the words I had memorized years ago. "I swear to stand by you, to obey and respect you, to give my strength to Fort Calmier and to the defenseless, to fight through my weakness."

I took a deep breath and turned around, bowing low to the court before me as everyone rose to their feet, thunderous applause and cheers ringing in my ears. Ice-cold Wind washed around me. I closed my hand around my great-grandfather's vial. The bell sounded in the next courtyard for the changing of the guards.

I saw Nick's Master off to the side, looking around in confusion. I scanned the crowd. Nick was gone.

Kane stepped forward, resting a hand on my shoulder. "Deep breath," he whispered. I sucked in a huge gulp of cold air, and the Wind died back to a gentle breeze.

The bell rang again.

I frowned. No one seemed to notice. The bell could barely be heard over the thundering crowd. Maybe that's why the guard rang it a second time.

The bell rang yet again.

The cheers turned to low murmurs, rippling out through the crowd. Then my stomach dropped.

The bell rang once again... and a wave of dark Water exploded over the battlements, extinguishing the torches, plunging us into darkness.

Someone screamed.

"They're coming over the southern wall!" A voice cried.

The crowd was shouting, bolting toward the armory and out into the next courtyard, toward the southern battlements. Then a soldier appeared on the rampart, his uniform the sharp red-on-black of the Ealdra.

Four

I STOOD FROZEN TO the platform deck, my heart pounding in my ears. The dark wave of Water died, running off the battlements. *Ealdra.* The courtiers warned me... *But we had thrown up extra defenses.* King Rehynall moved past me, raising his arms, shouting battle orders. Master Kane's sword was drawn. A guard rushed up the steps, his face streaked in dirt and blood, his sheath empty, his sword gone. King Rehynall whirled around.

"*Ealdra,*" the guard gasped. "We didn't see them coming."

"Get to safety, My King," Master Kane said firmly. King Rehynall's hand closed over my shoulder, gripping me tight.

He bent down and whispered, "*Hide!*" He spun around, and the lords followed him back into the castle, leaving Kane and I alone in the ceremonial courtyard. Everyone else had left for their defense posts. The air was heavy, every sound echoing off the stone. Wind whispered across the walls.

"Hey, Jackson!" came a call. A tall, scruffy man seemed to melt out of the southern wall, drawing his sword. He wore leather armor and was dressed in raggedy grays and browns, not the crisp red and black of the Ealdra.

"Run," Kane ordered. "Get to the armory. Find your bow."

I leapt, my shaking hand fumbling for my sword hilt. *The Ealdra knew my name.* Six more soldiers appeared out of the walls between me and freedom, the telltale fog of sorcery curling across the stone beneath them.

The tall man shook his head, raising his sword. "I don't think running is your best option," he said with a menacing grin. "Are you scared? Good thing you got your Master to protect you!" He roared in laughter.

My fingers closed around my sword hilt, and I drew the dark, Damascus blade, ice-cold Wind whipping around me. *I had to run. I had to run.*

A boy stepped out from behind the man, his mismatched eyes that marked him as a Rangerian shining in victory. He was only a few years older than me.

"Orin, leave him!" the man growled. "He's mine."

"Nope. Don't think so."

The boy threw up his arms, and hot Wind slammed into me, sending me spinning off the platform. I slammed into a row of spectator benches, hit the ground, and dropped my sword. With a groan, I pushed myself up and brushed the gravel off my hands. Kane leaped off the platform, sword raised. The other man threw up his blade, and the metal clashed wildly.

"Jack!" Kane yelled, ducking as the sharp steel slashed the air above him. "Remember when I told you to relax? Well..." The Hunter spun and slammed his blade with all his force against Kane's, throwing my Master back against the platform. *"Don't!"*

The Hunter lunged and Kane rolled aside. I snatched my own weapon off the ground, my throat tightening in terror. I could feel the North Wind whipping my insides into pudding. My hands were shaking.

Then I focused on my sword. *I am Jackson Marcrombie. I am the Guardian of the North.* My insides unknotted and I looked up, my Wind now swirling out of control around me in a tornado. The boy, Orin, sprang forward, rising into the air on a swirling column of hot Wind and courtyard dust. I dove away, swinging my blade up in defense. He landed in front of me and slashed. I jerked away, landing on my back. Dust filled my nose and throat, gritty on my tongue.

Kane cried out in pain. I rolled to my feet, spinning to see him fall back against the platform. A cry rose in my throat. My mind was whirling. I saw his blade hit the ground. Then a scream tore straight through me as the Hunter turned around, his sword shining brilliant red, and my Master collapsed at his feet.

Wind exploded from me. Orin blasted backward and hit the southern wall, coming to rest, motionless, at its base. The Wind picked me up, tearing straight through me in a hurricane. I dropped to my knees, the Ealdra Rangerian's dark Water trickling off the walls, flooding the courtyard. I planted my hands on the ground, my breath rushing through my lungs. Frost bristling over the benches, turning the Water that coated the courtyard to ice. My hands trembled as I picked up my sword, my shoes crunching on the icy stone. I could taste blood in my mouth. I staggered toward Kane's still body.

The Hunter ordered the other ragged soldiers on into the castle and stepped in front of me, a grin spreading across his gruff face that towered above me. *Red, dripping off the end of his sword.*

"Come on, Jackson," He took a step forward. This was him. This was the Sheriff. I glanced around. *I had to get out. I had to run.* "I know someone who is *very* excited to meet you." His eyes drifted to the vial hanging around my neck. A thought clicked into place and my gaze lifted. *The walkway arching between courtyards.*

"Good try, *Sheriff!*" I yelled, the words tearing at my hoarse throat. I took one last glance at my Master's body and made a break for the staircase across the courtyard. Four Hunters stepped into my path as the Sheriff tore after me. I saw movement out of the corner of my eye and spun, swinging my sword wildly.

Nick jumped out of the way.

"Sorry!" I squeaked.

"Down!" he shouted. I dove for the ground. Lightning exploded over my head, arcing across the frost-covered stone.

"Nick!" I shouted in surprise.

"Run!" he yelled. The Sheriff pushed himself up, shaking the last bit of electricity out of his system, and roared in fury.

"This way!" I raced toward the staircase.

Nick followed. We tore up the stairs, the Hunters hot on our tails. Nick turned and shot a blast of Lightning at the roof. Stone crashed down, blocking us off from pursuit.

I slowed to a stop at the top of the stairs and doubled over, gasping, trembling with adrenaline and shock. *The Ealdra found me. They killed my Master.... I had only gotten my power five minutes before, I had only sworn to Master Kane five minutes before.* I could see through the rows of wide windows to the courtyards below. Ealdra soldiers in their sleek red and black uniforms poured through the courtyard. My mind was whirling, careening out of control.

"Come on!" Nick yelled. His shout snapped my mind into focus. "We need to get to the stables!" I shook my head of the cobwebs, pushed up the sleeves of my green tunic, and clenched my sword. *I could deal with the shock after. I had to get out.*

34

I took off after Nick, sprinting down the corridor. Another wave of Water crashed over the walls and rushed through the windows ahead of us, shattering the stone, pounding down the corridor.

An Ealdra Rangerian appeared, the Water twisting around his feet.

Nick skidded to a stop, catching me in the chest. He groaned. "Really?"

The Rangerian spotted us and broke into a run, the Water carrying him forward. I glanced over my shoulder. We had two ways out—through this water demon, or out the windows, twenty feet to the courtyard below.

I almost jumped out of my skin when the Rangerian slammed his hand into the wall and more stone shattered, shooting past me in a dark wave of Water.

"Jack, get back. And get out of the Water!" Nick pushed me behind him and took a step forward. *"Get out of the way, Daniel,"* he ordered the onrushing Rangerian, his voice ringing over the rushing Water and clash of battle outside.

The boy shook his head. "Afraid not."

He spun and threw his arms toward us. I made a leap for the window ledge. Water blasted overhead, rushing down the corridor. A jet of Lightning arced through the air. Daniel leaped up. Nick's Lightning hit, flashing across the Water in a wave of crackling light. My hair stood on end. I landed safe on the window ledge.

Daniel didn't stop. He hit the Water and lunged forward. Nick faced him, and their blades clashed in a shower of sparks.

Gathering myself, I jumped forward to Nick's aid, but I was too slow. Nick's sword suddenly flew from his hand, and Daniel slammed him back against the wall. A flash of fear arced through me. My legs stopped moving.

I was seeing it all again.

It was all happening again.

Nick jerked against Daniel's grip. I raised my sword and lunged forward with a shout, letting my muscles take over. Daniel threw out his hand. I dove aside, but not quickly enough. A powerful jet of Water slammed into my chest, hurling me back into the stone, just inches from the open window. I gasped, the air rushing from my lungs. Painfully, I pushed myself to my feet.

I saw Lightning spark in Nick's palms. There was a sudden flash of steel, and Nick gasped sharply. Blood streamed down his arm. He stopped struggling.

Daniel raised his hand, and churning Water swirled up in his palms. *"You're a traitor, Nicolas Krom,"* he hissed.

Red, streaming down Nick's leather jacket.

Fear grabbed my insides. I felt the North Wind begin to roil inside me, my hands shaking. Wind lifted Daniel's hair.

"Jack! Move!"

I spun to see Kara sprinting down the corridor toward us, her dark skin glowing in the light of the fiery inferno that surrounded her. Her sword was drawn, the Damascus steel seeming to flow molten in her flickering flames. She raised her weapon, and I dove off to the side. A jet of Fire blasted past me, heat searing my skin.

Daniel saw it coming and threw up a shield of Water. The Fire exploded against it, hot steam billowing through the corridor. Kara's sandy braids rippled in the heat. The force of the blast shoved Daniel down the corridor. Kara fell back, panting in exhaustion.

Daniel saw his chance. He pushed himself off the stone and raised his hands, foaming Water whipping around his feet.

Kara caught my eye. "Jack! Down the walkway. Your Peryton got himself free!" She took a step toward Daniel, heat shimmering around her.

"Kara, no!" I cried.

"I can't control it... you'd better run!" She dropped her sword and raised her arms, flames flashing around her.

"Jack, go!" Nick cried through gritted teeth. When I didn't move, he grabbed my arm and pulled me down the corridor. Fire and Water exploded in the narrow space, clouds of steam blocking Kara from my vision, leaving only flashes of her silhouette as her Fire lit the air.

Nick and I veered around the corner and down a walkway, where wings flashed past the windows. I glanced out to find the battle below had moved deeper into the castle, but the Sheriff, his Hunters, and Orin stood waiting. *Waiting for me.*

"Perry!" I shouted, clumsily sheathing my sword. Without thinking, I leaped out a window. My stomach dropped with the fall. Perry swooped up, catching me on his back.

"Whoo!" I shouted, grabbing at his antlers. It had actually worked! "Nick!" I yelled. My Peryton's brown wings burst open and we dove under the walkway. Nick saw us and took a flying leap. I slid forward onto Perry's shoulders. The instant Nick hit Perry's back, we shot upward. Nick grabbed at my sword belt, nearly toppling at the sudden acceleration.

"You good?" I yelled back. I couldn't understand Nick's response over the roar of the battle. It sounded angry, twinged with pain. We flew over the corridor where we'd left Daniel and Kara, as blasts of Fire and Water exploded from the windows. I tugged on Perry's antlers, and we banked hard, a fireball just missing us. I leaned forward, my Peryton responding to my slightest touch. Up, up, and over the walls we rose, as another wave of Ealdra Rangerians launched into battle, the pounding warning bell fading away into the distance.

Five

PERRY'S WINGS BEAT IN my ears. My head was ringing. I could taste blood. Pain rose in about six different places on my body as the adrenaline faded. We angled downward, landing in a small clearing among thick trees, out of range of the battle.

I slid off Perry and sank to the ground, my hands shaking and covered in someone's blood. Nick swung off and raised his hand, forming a flickering, electric light that cut through the darkness, casting our shadows against the rough bark of the trees.

Brush rustled behind us. I staggered to my feet, reaching for my sword, cold Wind whipping up in a gale around me.

"Stand down!" Nick's Master called, his hand raised as he stepped out of the trees, leading his own panting Peryton. Nick sighed in relief and leaned back against one of the trees. The Lightning in his hand died out with a faint spark as he clasped his hand over his shoulder, letting out a groan.

Master Bancroft ran to him.

"It was Daniel da Costa," Nick gasped.

His Master reached over and touched the back of his bloody shoulder.

"The blade didn't go all the way through. Sit down." Nick slid to the ground, and Bancroft pulled a roll of bandages from his Peryton's saddlebag.

An explosion sounded behind us from the castle. I covered my head with my hands on instinct. My boots were drenched from Daniel's Water, and every inch of my body throbbed. *My Master was dead... the Ealdra had found me... the Sheriff was here...*

"Jackson." Master Bancroft looked around. "Look at me!" I lowered my shaking hands. "Take a deep breath. You can't be blowing trees over. You're going to give away our location. Try to stay calm."

I closed my eyes. The Wind died down around me. Bancroft bent down, pulled off Nick's leather jacket, and began winding the bandage around his shoulder.

"Nick! *Jack!*" a voice shouted. I shot to my feet. Wind roared around me.

"Stay behind me," Bancroft ordered, standing up and drawing his sword. "And *keep calm.*" He shot a look at me.

"Wait! That's Natanian." Nick half-stood with a grunt, a blazing ball of electricity igniting in his free hand. "Over here!" he shouted into the forest.

Natanian stumbled into the light and fell to his knees, puffing. I rushed forward. Natanian grabbed my shoulder, and in the light of Nick's crackling orb, I could see his face gone pale, his eyes wide with fear.

"They're coming," he gasped. "They saw you leave. They're coming!" A chill shuddered down my spine.

"We need to go *now*," Bancroft said.

"Where's Kara?" I demanded, ignoring Nick's Master. "Did you see Kara?"

Natanian shook his head, "She chased that Water Rangerian into the castle. She went right into the thick of battle. After that, I don't know."

"*We need to go*," Bancroft repeated.

"*Karalie—*" I looked back toward the castle.

"Kara's recklessness fuels her control," Nick whispered hurriedly. "If anyone can survive this, she can."

"You're right." I swallowed. "Where's your Peryton?" I grabbed Natanian's arm.

"Jack—" he whimpered, yanking away, pressing his hand to his side. He swayed. *He was hurt.*

"What happened?" I eased him down to the ground.

Natanian looked up at me and smiled weakly. "Feels great, getting shot."

"Natanian..." I grabbed his wrist, pulling his hand away from his side. He had thrown on his armor in such a rush, he'd left a loose gap. That's where the arrow hit him. *"And you pulled it out?"* I almost shouted. His face continued to lose color. "He's not going to make it." I looked up at Bancroft, pleading for help.

"No." Bancroft stepped up, planting his hand on Natanian's chest. "You're injured, you go back."

"I can't go back," Natanian breathed. "They took it." His eyes met mine, despair and fear shining in his pale face. "I couldn't get to my Master. The Ealdra took the throne."

My chest was cold. "Help me get him up." My voice was dry, low. It wasn't a question. I wouldn't leave him behind. But I knew we had to go. *Fort Calmier, taken. My parents... Kara... the king...*

Bancroft knelt down. I crouched on the other side and we lifted Natanian up. A cry escaped through his teeth.

"Wait," Nick called. "I can try to slow the bleeding."

"Are you sure?" Bancroft asked.

Lightning crackled over Nick's fingers. "I have to try. Or he's going to die."

Bancroft ripped open the tear in Natanian's tunic where the arrow had hit. Nick stretched out his fingers, narrowing his eyes. Lightning collected in his palm, sparking across his hand. Natanian's breaths were coming short and fast, dark blood streaming down his side, staining his tunic. I looked away.

I smelled smoke. I felt Natanian's muscles tense. I heard him stifle his scream, clenching his teeth tight. His knees gave out. I opened my eyes, catching his weight before he dragged me to the ground. Nick stepped back, closing his fist over the flickering Lightning.

Natanian moaned in pain. Burn scars branched across his side, but he was no longer losing blood, the wound sealed.

Bancroft whistled to his Peryton, who trotted over obediently. We lifted Natanian up, and Bancroft swung on behind him, holding the boy tight. Natanian's face was deathly pale, his eyes closed. His fingers slowly spread across the Peryton's neck.

"I got him," Bancroft said. I slid onto my mount and pulled Nick up behind me.

"Where do we go?" Nick asked. I closed my fingers tight around Perry's antlers, his wings shifting beneath me. The din of battle dropped by the second as the Ealdra seized tighter hold over the castle where I had grown up.

I made a quick decision. "I have a great-aunt just across the Wyoming border. My great-grandfather's daughter. She's a nurse. She'll give us a safe house."

Six

I NERVOUSLY GLANCED OVER my shoulder, my boots creaking on the wooden porch. The dirt road leading to my Great-Aunt Isabel's house was dark. Our Perytons picked at grass in the ditch. The only light came from the flickering porch lamp above my head.

"Well, this isn't creepy at all," I muttered.

"Jack," Bancroft urged me on.

I raised my hand to knock. Wind whistled through the forest. The porch light flickered faster, then flared bright before fizzling out. Natanian let out a low groan. His head hung on his chest, his weight supported by Nick and Bancroft.

"Welp." I swallowed, and knocked on the door. When nobody answered, I banged again.

The door creaked open an inch. Dim light fell across our sad little group. "Hi! Nice and creepy tonight, isn't it, Aunt Isabel?" I said in a rush.

Her eyes went from me, to my sword, to Natanian behind me. She threw the door open. Bancroft and Nick pushed their way past me and into the house.

"In the living room," she said shortly.

I stepped inside, and she swung the door closed, bolting it shut. She pushed up her sleeves and grabbed an apron off its hook, quickly tying it on over her pajamas.

We moved into the living room, and Isabel flicked on the lights. Natanian gave a faint grunt at the sudden brightness. "Sorry," she muttered, grabbing a clean sheet out of the basket she had been folding and swung it over the sofa.

Bancroft and Nick eased Natanian down on his back. A moment later, Natanian gasped in pain, and every light in the room burst.

"I always forget you Rangerians' effect on electronics," Isabel said drily. "There are some candles in the kitchen. Top right drawer." Nick left for the kitchen.

In the gloom, Isabel quickly braided her graying hair, tucked it out of the way, and knelt down, fumbling with Natanian's armor. "How do you take this off?"

Bancroft bent down and unstrapped the armor, dropping it aside. Nick returned, carrying a handful of candlesticks.

"Any other electronics you don't want to short-circuit before I light these?" he asked Isabel.

"Just light them."

Nick closed his hand around the tips of the candles, and they burst into flame with a flash of Lightning. He jerked away, shaking his hand.

"You good?" I asked, taking half the candles from him.

Isabel looked around, "Did you burn yourself, Rangerian?" Nick shot her a glare.

Natanian suddenly jerked, breaking the seal Nick had made on his side. Blood streamed down his tunic. Isabel cut through the fabric and pulled it off to see his injury. Nick and I set the candles around him. I grimaced as light flashed across his wound. I quickly looked away.

"How long ago?" Isabel asked.

"Three hours," Nick answered.

"It looks like someone tried to cauterize it. Was that you?"

Nick ducked his chin. "It didn't work, did it?"

"Not well enough." Isabel shook her head, pressing her fingers to the injured boy's scarred skin. He recoiled in pain.

"Why did you bring him here?" She glanced up at me.

"Um..." I set down the last candle. "You were closest."

She stood up. "I need to call an ambulance."

"*No.*" Nick stepped forward. A low rumble of thunder sounded overhead. "Jack said you could heal him."

"I'm a nurse, not a sorcerer!"

Nick took a deep breath, "We need to stay low. If you take him in with a shot wound, the police will ask questions. And if they track Natanian back to you, they will find Jack. Then it's only a matter of time before the ones who did *this* are here."

"Who's after Jack?" Isabel snapped.

"Can you heal him?" I interrupted.

She sighed, bending down again. "It's incredibly hard to tell exactly what was damaged without risking further injury. You said he was shot?"

"An arrow," Nick answered.

"And you pulled it out?" she asked incredulously.

"He did. It was the shock of it all, I think." I sank down on an ottoman next to the wall. Its fabric was rough beneath my hands. I could smell the lingering scent of Aunt Isabel's dinner in the next room. The candlelight cast flicking shadows across Natanian's pale face.

"He's lost a lot of blood." Isabel pressed her fingers to his neck, feeling for his pulse. "I can try," she finally said. She looked up at Bancroft, "But if he gets worse, I *am* taking him to the hospital."

"Fair enough." Bancroft stood up.

Aunt Isabel nodded. "I'll get my stuff."

I sat against the wall in the living room, a thick, blue blanket pulled up over my knees. Grandpa's... no... *my* vial felt cold against my chest. The ceremony seemed a lifetime ago.

Aunt Isabel slid down the wall to sit beside me. She blew on the cup of tea curled in her hands, "How did Natanian get shot?"

I glanced across at my friend. He lay on the sofa, his skin pale, clean bandages covering the new stitches in his side. "There was an attack on Fort Calmier."

"Ealdra?"

"Yep."

Outside, a gentle breeze ruffled through the branches, and crickets sang from the shadows. I pulled the blanket up further as a shiver ran through me. I had known Natanian for years. Seeing him like this... these people would stop at nothing. First my Master Kane died, now Natanian was injured. *How many more would there be?*

"They knew who I was," I whispered. "They came looking for *me.*"

"Why *now?*" Aunt Isabel asked.

"My power manifested tonight." I pulled my vial from my tunic.

"My dad's necklace..." she whispered, and I opened my palm. The mist spun up into a tornado, spiraling in the tiny vial. Wonder filled her eyes. She looked up at me and smiled. "You're powerful."

"Not enough if *this* happens." I gestured at Natanian.

"That's not true."

"There weren't just Ealdra soldiers at the attack." The tornado in the vial exploded into mist. I let go, letting it swing back into my chest.

"What do you mean?" She took a sip of tea.

"There were... they looked like rogues. The Sheriff and his Hunters. They wanted my power. It's the only thing that makes sense with their timing."

Shock and worry flashed across her face. "What for?"

"I don't know." I exhaled, the cold breeze dying down around me. "The Ealdra also took the throne. Whatever they found, whatever they're planning... it's not just about my power. There's something bigger."

"Jack." My great-aunt moved closer, looking me right in the eyes. "This will always be a safe house." Her gaze lingered on my vial. "I understand. My dad always knew there was danger attached to that power."

I looked down at my hands. As much as this Rangerian power was a blessing, it carried the curse from the Golden Arrow. And that curse would always be strongest in the strongest among us. In True Borns like Grandpa. Like me. Yet, I was scared, no matter how much I tried to hide it.

She took another sip of her tea and looked across at the sofa. "Natanian is going to be fine." I sighed in relief. "You can stay as long as you need to."

"I don't know how much of that is up to me." I grinned. "If anyone is going to get antsy about keeping still, it's Natanian. I don't think he can stand staying in hiding while he recovers."

SEVEN

WHEN I WOKE UP in the morning, Nick was gone. Sunlight streamed through the window, and the birds were declaring many proclamations with much enthusiasm.

I threw off my blanket and moved over to check on Natanian. Great-Aunt Isabel entered through the kitchen with a bowl of steaming water and a roll of fresh bandages.

Natanian stirred and opened his eyes. "Do you like watching me sleep?" he mumbled. His voice was dry.

I started to defend myself. Then I laughed, "Did you know you bark in your sleep? You also started to grow furry ears, I *think*."

"Shut up." He glared at me. I grinned.

Aunt Isabel knelt down in front of him, "How do you feel?"

"Weak, dizzy, a little... *ruff* around the edges." He shot me a smirk.

I winced, "Oh, that one was bad."

"What?" Aunt Isabel glanced between us.

I grimaced. "You don't want to know."

"It's going to take you a few days to get back the blood you lost," she warned.

Natanian pushed back the blanket to see the bandages, "How bad is it?"

She shrugged, "I've seen worse."

"How have you seen *worse?*" I demanded.

"I work in the emergency room, Jack."

"Oh."

Isabel sat back. "I'm going to replace the bandages. Jack, there's a new set of clothes on the kitchen table for you."

"But I—" I glanced down at my Áccyn uniform, the mottled green tunic dirty and torn. She had a point. I went into the kitchen. There was a brand-new pair of jeans, a tee shirt, and a sweatshirt folded on the kitchen table, still with their tags attached.

I emerged from the bathroom, tugging the sweatshirt down over my belt. The jeans were a size too big, but anything would blend in better around here than my medieval, battle-worn tunic.

I saw a shadow shift out of the corner of my eye. I crossed back into the kitchen and pushed open the patio door. Nick was leaning against the railing, looking out through the forest. He'd cleaned up, at least. And he was wearing a new pair of jeans that Isabel had bought for him sometime this morning. *His* fit him.

"Fine weather we're having, sir," I said by way of greeting. "I see my aunt figured your size better than mine." I tugged on my baggy jeans.

He shrugged, "I guess she likes me better."

"She gonna adopt you?"

"Maybe."

I leaned on the railing beside him. "What are you doing out here?"

"Just... went for a walk."

"Uh-huh. Sure. *You* went for a w—"

"How does it feel?" he interrupted.

"–walk," I finished. "Huh?"

"Knowing they're out there?"

"Who, the interrupter gang?"

"Sorry to remind you." He patted me on the back. An electric shock jumped from his hand.

"Dude!" I flinched.

"Oops." He grinned.

"Every time." I shook my numb arm.

"Do you think..." He gestured out to the trees. "Do you think they know where we are?"

"How could they?" I gripped the porch railing, an uneasy feeling crawling in my stomach.

Isabel led Natanian through the screen door and gently sat him on the porch chair. She patted my shoulder. "Don't let him bleed out, okay?" She walked back into the house.

"Yeah. Right." I looked down at Natanian, his blond hair sticking every-which-way.

"Wow, it's a bit tense out here," he said, catching the curt tone in my voice.

I cleared my throat, watching as a chipmunk sprinted across the ground and dove under a rotting log.

Natanian looked from me to Nick, waiting for an explanation.

"How did they know who I was?" I finally blurted out. "What do they even want with me?" Wind whistled through the trees.

"Maybe that's why," Bancroft answered, climbing up the steps onto the porch. "You're strong. Your power is strong."

I took a deep breath, trying to calm the twisting cold inside me. "Yeah, I can't control it."

"You will." He stopped next to me and pointed at my chest. "Your power is the strongest I've ever seen this close to its Manifestation. From what Nick told me, what you did in the courtyard shouldn't have been possible. You shouldn't have been able to knock anyone off their feet, least of all hurl a Hunter that far into the wall. That kind of force takes years of training to accomplish. At the Manifestation, your power is always just strong enough to be a nuisance, to do... *that*." He gestured to the swaying branches around us.

"Well, maybe it's because Kane..." I trailed off, the painful, violent memory threatening to burst to the surface.

Bancroft sighed. "No, I've seen that too—a newly-manifested Rangerian acting under trauma.

That wasn't it." He looked me right in the eyes. "Your Master is gone. You have to learn control if you want a *chance* at getting away from the Ealdra, and the Sheriff they commissioned, apparently."

I glanced at Nick. He nodded.

"Will you help me?" I asked his Master.

Bancroft's eyes shifted over the deck, over Nick spinning his ring as he leaned against the railing, and held out his arm, "I swear to stand by you, to defend you, to train you by sword and power until you are Master."

I closed my hand around the armor on Bancroft's forearm and looked up into his eyes. "I swear to stand by you, to obey and respect you, to give my strength to..." I cleared my throat and laughed. "...*whatever* court we end up in, to the defenseless, and to fight through my weakness."

Eight

BANCROFT PACED AROUND ME, his boots crunching on the forest floor. His graying hair was pulled back in a short ponytail to keep it from being blown by my Wind. The sun was bright today, streaming through the trees above. Up on the porch, Nick leaned against the railing, watching. Natanian sat back against a log a few feet away. I could smell Aunt Isabel's breakfast cooking inside the house.

"A Rangerian's powers are harder to control the stronger his emotions are," Bancroft explained. "Whenever you are angry, afraid, nervous, or even excited, they will surface with or without your will. *Unless you know how to control them.* You are True Born. The stronger your power is, the more difficult it is to harness, and the longer it takes for you to master it. So..." He stopped and turned to face me, raising his long sword. "How far are you willing to go to stay alive?"

I yawned. "Do I have to answer that now? Too philosophical for this early in the morning."

"Wrong answer. How far are you willing to go to stay alive?"

"Is this a test?"

"The answer's forty-two," Natanian whispered.

"Wow, thanks," I called back.

"You need to know your limits, Jackson." Bancroft took a step toward me. "The Hunters came for you. The Ealdra broke our peace. They captured Fort Calmier." He lowered his sword and sighed. "I believe this was all done from the inside."

It felt like someone had punched me in the gut.

"Whoa." Natanian sat back.

Nick straightened. "You mean... *the spy.*"

"What?" I looked between Nick and Master Bancroft. "You think the spy is real?" Bancroft nodded. "And *you* knew about this?" I pointed an accusing sword at Nick.

Bancroft rested the tip of his blade on the ground. "Three weeks ago, a group of soldiers went missing the very night they left on a mission. The only ones who knew they'd left were *inside* Fort Calmier. Two weeks before that, there was an attempt on King Rehynall's life. *In the middle of the day*. The only way the assassin could have gotten in was through help from the inside. One of the court." He eyed me.

I swallowed. "You don't think it was *me?*"

I saw a flicker of trepidation in Natanian's eyes. "That's crazy," he said weakly.

"No, you aren't the spy." Nick shook his head. "If King Rehynall suspected you, do you think he would have stood up there with you during your Manifestation? When your power was most chaotic? Any strike could easily have been passed off as an accident."

My heart pounded in a cascade of shock. "Thought about this much, Nick?"

Nick shrugged, "It happened before. With King Balhuntingdon."

My heart jumped another beat.

"No one except the council knew about this," Bancroft said. "The king didn't want to raise tension.

Announcing the presence of a spy would only turn the court against itself."

"So... what exactly does this have to do with me?"

"It can be no coincidence that the Sheriff infiltrated Fort Calmier and the Ealdra launched an attack on the very night of your Manifestation ceremony."

A cold chill ran down my spine. I hadn't thought of *that*. Of course. Everyone in the castle knew where I was at that moment. Any one of them could have tipped off the Ealdra. I might have to fight against one of my own court... *one of my own friends.* The Sheriff had teamed up with the Ealdra, and one of our Áccyn soldiers had let them in.

Nick's Thunder rumbled overhead and he rubbed his hands, calming his power. I wasn't just escaping from the Sheriff. I was fleeing an entire nation of Robin Hood's descendants.

"Breathe, Jackson," Bancroft murmured.

I exhaled. A cold chill was whistling through the trees, and my deep breath didn't do anything to calm it down.

"If anyone saw us leave, saw the direction we took, *and knows you,*" Natanian said nervously, "we might not be safe."

"So." Bancroft regained my attention. "How far are you willing to go to stay alive?"

I took another deep breath. The truth was, I had no idea. Was I going to be able to fight someone from Fort Calmier? Possibly one of my own friends?

He lifted his sword from the ground and leveled the blade at me. "Controlling your power will not be easy. It takes work. Lots of work. And you do not have much time."

"I got it," I muttered. "Let's go. Let's get started. How tough can it be?" My hands had gone cold. I didn't want to be here. I didn't want to be running for my life from those people. If the spy *did* know where I had gone, I didn't want to put Aunt Isabel in danger.

Most of all, I didn't want to have to face a friend who wanted me dead.

NINE

"*F*OCUS!" BANCROFT SHOUTED, AND the flat of his sword hit my shoulder again. I clenched my teeth, drawing my thoughts away from the pain.

"Well, maybe if you stop hitting me," I muttered under my breath.

"What?" He stared at me from under his thick, graying eyebrows.

"I'm *trying*." My cold Wind began to die down again.

"Need some help?" Nick asked. He flicked his wrist, and a bolt of Lightning shot toward me.

I jumped out of the way. "Not you too!" Bancroft's blade hit the side of my leg. *"Guys!"* I closed my hands into fists, forcing the twisting power into my control. Bancroft swung, knocking my legs out from under me. I fell flat on my back, and a blast of cold Wind burst away from me. Aunt Isabel caught her can of soda on the porch railing before it hit the ground.

Bancroft chided, "Try harder."

I coughed, air rushing back into my lungs. The branches rustled off to my right. The hair rose on the back of my neck. That reaction was too far away to have come from my Wind. I pushed myself to my feet and stared through the trees into the shadows. I gulped.

"What is it?" Natanian froze at his post on the porch.

"Hey, Master Bancroft," I warned. "There's someone there." I unsheathed my sword. Natanian dropped a stick he'd been fiddling with and did the same. Nick came slowly down the steps, watching.

I saw a shift in the shadows, a faint dark form of a girl. Then a glint of steel appeared in the gloom, and I heard the familiar hum. Nick and I dove back. An arrow slammed into the porch, the black shaft sinking three inches deep in the wood. The arrow stood, quivering. I whipped around, but the archer was gone.

Nick took off through the trees.

"Nicolas!" Bancroft shouted.

I glanced at Natanian. His face paled. He shook his head and rocked back, pressing his hand to his bandaged side. "Not doing that."

I ran after Nick, weaving through trees and leaping over fallen logs as Bancroft yelled something unintelligible. I slashed through a tangle of brush with my sword and caught a glimpse of the archer's slim build and deep green cloak through the trees, far ahead of us. I slid to a stop beside Nick at the edge of the woods, panting. The Dark Archer had vanished into the shadows.

We found ourselves on the edge of a highway. Cars roared past, kicking up puffs of dust. Nick cursed and slammed his hand against a tree. Lightning arced up the bark. He jerked back, rubbing his hand on his jacket.

"How did she find us?" I shoved my blade back in its sheath, the worst possibility running through my mind. *The spy.*

"We should leave," was all Nick said.

"Jackson!" Bancroft shouted through the trees. "Nicolas!" He emerged from the woods and slowed to a stop. "Whoever it was wasn't here to kill us."

"Sorry, Master." Nick turned around.

"Sorry...." I echoed.

"I don't think it was a Hunter." Bancroft held out a folded note to me. "This was on the arrow shaft." I took the letter. My name was printed across the front in sharp black letters. Nick moved closer as I tore it open. The letter was written in a different handwriting:

WEST WIND HAS BEEN SECURED.

WE FOUND NORTH.

It was signed with a pair of crossed daggers.

"The Sheriff," Nick whispered and grabbed the letter, flipping it over, "This is dated a week ago." He looked up at me.

My stomach dropped. This confirmed it. They were hunting me for my power. And I was the only one left. Something they had found... they would need the four Winds to secure it.

What would they do when they were done? They wouldn't need me anymore. This was going to end with me dead, if I was caught.

"We should leave," Nick repeated, glancing back up at the highway. *"Now."*

Frost curled beneath my feet as I sprinted through the forest, cold North Wind trailing behind me. Fear knotted my stomach. This was it. They had no one else to get. The entire troop of Hunters was looking for me.

Bancroft threw open the back door, making Aunt Isabel jump. Nick and I followed him inside.

Natanian came around the corner. The color had returned to his face, but he was still moving slowly. "Did you find her?" He looked worried.

"If this archer found us, the Hunters won't be far behind," Bancroft said. "We're leaving."

Aunt Isabel dropped the tray of tea on the counter and started grabbing food for us from the cabinet.

Natanian moved forward. "Right now?"

"Now." Bancroft picked up Natanian's sword belt leaning against the wall and handed it to him, then left to help Isabel.

Natanian's hands shook. I stepped forward, grabbed the scabbard from him, and strapped it around his waist. He winced at the sudden stab of pain.

"Sorry."

"It's fine."

"Get the Perytons," Bancroft ordered. Nick nodded and left to round them up. I followed Natanian out the back door and down the stairs to the forest floor. Bancroft and Aunt Isabel stepped out the door behind us. Nick appeared a moment later, leading the two Perytons. Natanian struggled up on Perry and I climbed up in front of him.

Aunt Isabel gave Natanian a large bag. "There's food, water, and your dressings for a week."

"Be careful," Bancroft told her, settling down on his mount, Nick swinging up behind him. "If the signs are true, the Sheriff or Ealdra will be here in a matter of days."

Isabel stepped back. "Don't worry. I will."

"Where to?" I asked the others, my fingers tightening on Perry's antlers. His wings shifted beneath me.

"We'll figure it out on the way," Bancroft answered.

"Jack," Aunt Isabel took a satchel from her shoulder and held it up to me. "This was your great-grandfather's. I thought you might like to have it."

My fingers closed around the leather strap. My great-grandpa's name, *Rowan Tyler*, was embroidered in the lining. I traced the letters. "Thank you." I smiled down at her. She squeezed my hand one last time.

I swung the satchel over my shoulder, wheeled Perry around, and launched into the afternoon sky.

TEN

ISABEL TYLER STOOD AT the window, her hand bunched up around the curtain. The Master had been right. Two nights later, and they were here. She could see shapes outside her house, drifting through the forest trees. The curtain swung shut. She crossed into the kitchen, the sound of her feet on the wood echoing through the quiet house.

She pulled her pot of soup off the stove and reached behind the oven for a short steel sword. A loud knock came at the door. She jumped, spinning around. She breathed out, brushed the loose strands of hair from her face, and slid the blade inside her robe. If it came to violence, there it would end. For better or for worse. Her father had taught her how to wield this sword. She would not betray her nephew. She would never be too old to defend her family.

She tightened her robe and crossed to the door. Her fingers rested a moment on the cold metal of the lock, then she turned it with a *click*, and pushed the door open.

A tall, scruffy man, dressed in fraying clothes and leather armor, stood on her doorstep. The porch light cast dark shadows across his face. He put a large hand on the door frame and thrust a foot forward, flashing the hilt of his long sword.

"Hello, m'lady." He gave Isabel a short bow. "May we come in? It's awful windy out 'ere." He took a step forward. She subtly shifted, blocking his path. He frowned, his knuckles tightening on his sword hilt. "Soup smells good," he said, unamused.

She gave him a gentle smile. "May I ask who you are? What brings you out here?" Her eyes drifted past him. She could see only two other Hunters behind him, lingering out on the dirt road. One, a man with a long, blond beard, appeared a little drunk. The other stood perfectly still, his mismatched eyes watching her. In the light of the porch lamp, she could see he was young and thin, a boy a few years older than Jack.

The man before her leaned in. "My name is Androuet. And my friends and I are hungry." He nodded at the others.

Isabel suspected that the rest of the Hunters must be circling around the house toward the back door. *They weren't acting like bounty hunters. They weren't doing this for the money.*

Then for what?

"I'm sorry," she said firmly, "I only have food for one."

"That'll do fine." He shoved the door open and pushed past her. She wrinkled her nose. He smelled like he hadn't showered in a week; stale liquor and musk hung around him, clinging to his fraying uniform.

Androuet motioned to the two Hunters to follow. The boy's eyes caught Isabel's as he passed, and he hesitated.

"He's not here," she whispered. Her fingers tightened around her robe belt. The boy didn't make a move for his sword. He didn't need to. He was trapped here, with the Hunters.

And trapped animals were always the most dangerous.

"Orin!" Androuet shouted from the kitchen, where he and his Hunters were rifling through the cupboards.

The boy ignored him, moving closer to Isabel. "Then where is he?" he demanded, his voice low.

"I don't know."

He slammed the front door shut, grabbed Isabel's arm, and dragged her into the kitchen. He threw her forward. She hit the table, re-injuring the bruise on her hip. She slowly pushed herself up. This boy was much stronger than he looked.

Androuet dropped the spoon in the soup and turned around, wiping his beard on his sleeve. "What's it going to take, m'lady Isabel?" He moved toward her.

"I don't know what you're talking about."

The drunk Hunter stood up from his seat at the table. "You're lyin'."

"He was here." Sheriff Androuet drew his long sword. "Jackson. And his... friends. Where did he go?"

"They didn't say," she told the boy... *Orin*. He was the one to worry about. This Sheriff and other Hunters were nothing compared to what he could do.

Androuet sheathed his sword. "Now, that's better. Who was he traveling with?"

"Two of his friends from court. And one of their Masters."

"Good, good. Now, I know when you're telling the truth." He glanced at Orin and back at Isabel. "You're his aunt, right? You were Rowan Tyler's daughter."

"That was a long time ago."

He laughed, and his stinking breath washed over Isabel. "Not that long ago."

"We found West Wind," Orin spoke up. "Jackson is the last one."

"I know," she said calmly.

"You *know?*" Androuet took a step back. "How?" Whatever enjoyment was left in his eyes vanished into the grime that clouded his face.

"The letter." She reached behind her and slid the letter off the table, holding it up to him.

He snatched it away. "West Wind has been secured," she recited. "We found North." Sheriff Androuet gritted his teeth, ripped the note in half, and threw it to the floor.

Orin's eyes lingered on the fallen letter. "He knew we were coming."

"Who gave it to you?" Androuet shouted.

"It came from an anonymous messenger," Isabel said slowly. "I don't know who she was." She looked up at him, frowning. "But..." *Here was something. Here was perhaps the one card she held.* "...neither do you."

"A stranger." Orin moved forward.

"It was an archer." Her hand gripped the hem of her robe. *Not yet.* "They couldn't catch her. The Dark Archer, they called her."

"How did this archer find him?" Androuet demanded.

"I don't know," she repeated.

Orin's voice took on a note of exasperation. "You know Jackson's world. You were Rowan Tyler's daughter, which means they all *know* you've known of our world for years. Which means this place—" He drew out his dagger and slammed it into the table beside her, the blade sinking deep into the wood.

"—would make the *perfect* safe house. Jackson knew we were coming. The *archer* found you. How?"

She swallowed and stepped away from the table, lowering her voice, turning to the young Rangerian. "They don't know what happened to you, Orin," she whispered. "Some think you're dead. You're South Wind, right?"

He stopped. "How did you know?"

"You haven't any idea who the archer is, do you?"

"Enough!" Androuet shouted. He shoved Orin aside. A hot breeze ruffled through Orin's hair as his hands clenched into tight fists. But he didn't do anything, steeling the rising fury behind his eyes.

Then Androuet drew his sword and made a move toward Isabel. She slipped her blade from her robe and pushed herself away from the table, raising the weapon before her.

Androuet stopped. "You can tell *me,* or I can bring you to my client." His voice was rough and low. "He's much less reasonable." The Sheriff winked. "Now, *where is Jackson?"*

She told herself this would happen.

The back door slammed open. More Hunters moved inside.

Isabel counted six sets of footsteps. *She had prepared herself for this.* The Wind twisting around Orin grew stronger. He dropped his hands and it whipped up into a small tornado. *If it came to violence, there it would end.*

She took a deep breath, and gripped her sword tight. "I can't tell you that."

Eleven

I JERKED AWAKE. RAIN pattered in the canopy of leaves above me. The fire had died out. Nick stepped out of the trees, carrying an armful of firewood. The rain began to die down, the faint glimmers of starlight shining through the trees.

Nick dumped the pile of wood down against a tree and grabbed two of the logs, moving over to the dead fire. He glanced at me, pushing his hair out of his face. I stood up, stretching my stiff muscles, and plopped down in front of the campfire. He set the logs on the ashes and crouched down.

"Not very good at this whole 'surviving in the woods' thing, are we?" I yawned.

He glanced up at me. "You probably want to move back a bit." I scooted back a good five feet. Nick spread his fingers over the wood as if warming his hands. Instead, Lightning flashed over his skin, crisscrossing his face with flickering shadows. The electricity shot down to the dry logs. The bark began to smoke, thin tendrils rising through Nick's cold, flickering light. The wood burst into flame and Nick jerked back.

"Nice." I grabbed a stick off the ground and chucked it at him. He caught it in a flash of Lightning. Ash drifted from his fingers. "Alright." I yawned, turning back to the fire. "That was a little more violent than was necessary. But cool," I admitted.

Nick sat down, crossing his legs on the forest floor. The darkness in his eyes faded to a smile.

I looked around. Natanian was awake. He dropped his blanket off his shoulders and sat down between us. "That looked easy," he quipped.

Nick leaned back, "Well, you do it next time." Natanian reached for the fire, Ice curling up his fingers. Nick slapped his arm away. "Hey. Hands off."

"If Kara was here, she would show you how it's *really done*." He grinned at Nick, then shot a glance in my direction.

I laughed. "She'd have no problem out here." Sadness started to creep over me. I'd grown up with Kara... when her Fire manifested six months ago, she seemed to get a new wave of confidence. All her sarcasm turned up to ten....

I sighed. The flames flared with a *pop,* sending a cloud of sparks that twisted together up into the night sky before they disappeared, fading into the stars. The clouds were almost gone, the sky clear, the stars bright. I suddenly remembered the satchel Aunt Isabel had given me—my great-grandfather's. I reached behind me and grabbed it from where it leaned against a tree.

"What's that?" Natanian moved closer.

"Probably a dragon egg," I answered.

Nick looked up in curiosity. "Doubtful."

"You're right. It's probably a tiny elf." I flipped open the satchel, running my fingers along the embroidered name on the hem. *Rowan Tyler.*

"I was thinking more of a tiny *cursed* elf," Nick elaborated.

"Ah-ha!" I yanked out a stack of photographs and set the satchel aside.

"Well that was anticlimactic." Natanian shrugged and sat back.

"What are they?" Nick asked.

"They're... of my grandpa." I tilted my head. I recognized his eyes, his smile. I'd never actually seen photos of him this young.

The first was a picture of three young men, dressed in their mottled green Áccyn uniforms, swords strapped to their sides. Two of the soldiers carried longbows, and a quiver sat at their feet. The guy on the right had to be my grandpa.

"Is he as clumsy as you?" Nick asked. Natanian waved at him to shut up.

Grandpa Tyler had the same hair as me, the same chin. His blue and brown eyes sparkled even in this old photo, the exact same shades as mine. I saw the glint of a chain around his neck. I touched my chest, feeling that same cold, silver chain against my skin. He must not have been much older than me in this picture, if he still needed the vial to control his power. He was True Born too, which meant he, too, had probably been in danger wherever he went. Those of us who carried the power of the Golden Arrow curse the strongest... who had the power of the eleven guardians... we True Borns seemed to lead a trail of bad. Everything was stronger around us. Those who sought our power sent their best-of-the-best after us.

They found me. I got away from Fort Calmier, and the Hunters found me. I couldn't escape. I was on the run. I took a deep breath, calming the thoughts swirling in my head. The cold breeze around me died to a gentle whisper. What would happen if the Sheriff caught up to me? He needed me... or maybe my power... but how far would he go to get me?

I looked back down at the picture. There was no fear in my grandpa's eyes. I had hardly been able to shake that fear since my Manifestation. But that same courage he'd held, that same blood flowed in me now. That same excitement.

I flipped to the next picture. I saw Grandpa Tyler at about the same age, sword drawn, raised in front of him. He was giving a death-stare into the camera, his mismatched eyes more pronounced than ever. I could still hear his voice in my head. *Jackson Marcrombie, the Great Guardian of the North.* Is that what they called *him*? The 'Great Guardian of the North'?

The next photo was of him sitting on a log in the forest, in front of Fort Calmier, beside a girl... my great-grandma. There was also another of the boys from the first photo. Grandpa Tyler was older here, probably eighteen or nineteen. A deep scar crossed his arm. But his eyes sparkled.

I looked past him, to the torch-lit battlements of Fort Calmier rising above the trees, shrouded by the fog that showed remnants of the sorcery used to keep the castle hidden. He walked the same halls I walked, ate in the same hall in which I ate. He served his court.

The fire sparked and crackled, the only sound on the edge of these woods. I tugged the chain from beneath my shirt and gripped the vial tight, feeling the coolness in my hand, seeing the gray mist swirl beneath my fingers. The Hunters would still come after me, so long as the Ealdra held their cards. I didn't know what those cards showed. I didn't know why they needed my power.

But I was strong. Robin Hood's blood flowed through my veins. I had the power of the North Wind inside me. I would learn to control it. I would stand up against these monsters, no matter what the fear screaming inside me said.

I looked up. Golden light was breaking on the horizon, shooting across the sky in fiery rays. "Look," I said quietly, "the sunrise."

"Come on," Natanian said. "I have an idea for you to begin learning control." He painfully stood up and motioned for me and Nick to follow him.

I dropped the photos back in Grandpa's satchel and slung it over my shoulder, then strode after them across the forest floor.

Twelve

WE EMERGED FROM THE tree line. A wide river twisted down the hillside before us. Cold wind whistled past. Natanian moved forward, kneeling beside the river bank.

"Light 'em up, Nick."

"Um... are you sure about this?" I took a cautious step backward as Nick moved forward.

He knelt on the river bank and rubbed his hands together. Sparks of electricity flashed up his arms. He touched his fingers to the surface, and Lightning burst through the water. A cloud of steam billowed up. Nick jerked back. Natanian threw out his hand, freezing the steam into tiny Ice crystals, holding them, hovering, in midair.

"Blow it away," he encouraged, a mischievous grin spreading across his face. I shivered in the cold.

"You gonna shock me too?" I asked Nick. He raised his hands and stepped back, smiling at the look on my face. I shook my head. "Love this." I breathed out and raised my hands. I thrust them toward the snow cloud. Nothing happened, other than a few crystals curling away with the ever-present breeze around me.

"You can't learn to move what you can't even grasp," came a voice. I turned around. Bancroft strode out of the tree line. Natanian dropped his arms, and the Ice crystals drifted down, settling on the grass at his feet. Another gust of Montana wind whistled past. I breathed in the crisp, cold air, fueling the energy in my chest. My own small vortex picked up speed.

"Can't I just run at things?" I offered. "Spin things away, you know?"

"Sit down."

"Yes, Master." I sighed, glancing at Natanian with a shrug.

I sat with my eyes closed on the cold grass on the cold ground for what seemed like hours, trying to calm myself enough to bring my power under total control.

"Remind me again why we're up in *Montana?*" Natanian groaned at Bancroft, his breath puffing in little clouds. I tried to shut their conversation out, focusing on my own breath, on the cold tingle in my chest.

"Jackson's power is strongest out in the open, in the cold, where the Wind is unbound by trees or stone. Here is the perfect place for him to train. If he can learn to control his power when he is the strongest, it will be easier when he is weakest. It's the perfect place for him to learn to contain it."

I took a deep breath, spreading my fingers in the grass.

"Say, buried alive," Nick explained sarcastically.

I cracked one eye open, grabbed a handful of dry grass, and threw it at him.

"Again!" Bancroft shouted. I clenched my fists tight, shifting my weight on the dry ground. Nick sat a little ways away, watching. Natanian flashed me a mischievous smirk through his hovering cloud of snow.

I focused on the crystals again, reaching for the ice-cold feeling in my chest, and thrust my hand forward. I took a deep breath, and tried again. And again. Nothing happened. *Great shock.*

I was standing on the top of the hill by camp, the river rushing past before me. There was nothing around us for miles.

"Feel that power inside you," Bancroft said, "Let it flow through every inch of your body." He was pacing around me again. I stared at that stupid cloud of snow hovering around Natanian, and felt the familiar cold chill race out from my chest to my fingers. "Hold onto it. Don't let it go."

"I'm *holding onto it,*" I muttered through gritted teeth, glaring at the cloud.

"Don't mess up," Nick encouraged.

I concentrated with all my might on that stupid cloud, ignoring Nick, blocking out everything else. Just like I had done every other day.

"Just don't think about it," Natanian suggested.

"Easy for you to say."

"Any time now," Natanian needled me.

"Can you all just shut up and let me focus?" I hissed, "Please?"

Natanian laughed. "You're doing terrible." Bancroft shot him a glare. "I mean great," he muttered, the cloud of snow rising a little higher around him.

I closed my eyes. *Come on, Jack. You can do this. Grandpa Tyler had done it.* I breathed out. I could see him again in my memory. I felt the cold ground beneath my feet, the wind against my skin. I smiled to myself. The memory of his voice rose, telling the grand tales he claimed were of Robin Hood—which I was realizing, more and more, were half his own adventures. I could hear the rushing stream, feel the cold mist on my skin, rushing down my lungs. *One day,* he said.

I thrust my hand forward. The cloud of Snow burst apart. Natanian's eyes widened in surprise. He slowly lowered his hands. The Snow flew in streaks across the hill, melting into the air behind him.

Gray mist curled down my arms.

"*YES!*" I shouted.

After that, things started happening much faster. I could manipulate that stupid cloud of Ice however I wanted. Bancroft would chuck sticks at me to deflect. Natanian turned up his power, sending a spray of tiny Ice shards. I had to throw up a shield to stop them. But I could only control small things. If I tried anything against a person, all I would accomplish would be ruffling their hair.

The hardest part was when I got spooked or nervous or scared, or even laughed too hard, we would end up with a small tornado of air conditioning around us.

Thirteen

W E HAD MOVED AGAIN, keeping on the run from the Hunters. We were up in Canada... I think.

I sat with the others around a roaring campfire we'd actually managed to keep going this time. Tall, dark trees rose around us, their branches twisting into the air, glistening with frost.

I lounged back in the grass, watching the others. Nick sat between Natanian and me. Bancroft sat on the other side of the fire, running a sharpening stone across his blade. I watched as the sparks drifted up from the tips of the flames to fade in the darkness. The flickering shadows made it look almost as if the branches of the trees were grabbing at the drifting sparks.

I wonder how my grandpa had spent the first two weeks after getting his power. We had been at peace with the Ealdra for years, or at least there were no attacks, so he probably wasn't running for his life. *His Master probably hadn't died the first night.*

"What's wrong?" Nick asked.

I started, looking up. "Nothing."

"No, I know that look." Natanian sat back.

I laughed nervously. "What look is that?"

"The one you get when a haunting memory surfaces," he answered slowly. This got Bancroft's interest.

I shifted uneasily, "Yeah, I was remembering Master Kane. How... do you know what *'haunting memory'* looks like, Natanian?"

"Well, you know..." He touched his side absentmindedly, the spot where he'd been shot. "Never mind." He turned back around. "Let's talk about something else."

"Is there something we should know?" Bancroft asked.

"Or something only wee night elves should know?" I teased, trying to lighten the mood.

A small smile briefly crossed his face. "It's something only my Master and the recruiter know..."

He looked away. "How they found me," he finished quietly. He leaned back against a tree, "Sorry. Don't worry about it. I just remembered... when you made that look." He waved at me.

Bancroft set down his sharpening stone, wiped his blade on a clean cloth, and sheathed it. "Natanian, tell us what happened." I leaned forward. Nick looked up, curious.

Natanian hesitated, then sank against the tree. "I'm from northern Maine. But you know that... It's cold there, where I grew up. Very cold. So when my power manifested... I didn't realize what had happened for two days."

The surroundings faded around me. Natanian had been so distant when we'd first met....

"It was the middle of winter. We had a fireplace, the kind that looks as big as a room when you're little. I got in a fight with my friend over something stupid." He shook his head, "But it made me furious. I stormed into the living room, kicked the table, and the fire went out. Ice had covered everything. I remember thinking *that* was impossible. That's when I got suspicious."

"Suspicious?" I cried. "You turned your house into an ice rink!"

"Yeah, well, I was fourteen and scared. How do you think it felt out in *that* world? I had no idea about all this." He waved his hand around.

"Fair enough." I moved my sword out of the way and leaned against a tree.

"Well, the next day on the dock, I ran into this friend again and we had a second argument. This one was really bad. I remember hearing the wood under me crack, I remember seeing the ice spread across the water, then *boom.* The dock under him shattered, and he fell ten feet onto solid ice. The winter ice had been broken up that morning. But now it went all the way down to the marina bed. I *felt* it inside me then. I *knew* I had made that happen.

"Then I did something I shouldn't have." He tossed a rock on the fire and the haunting look fell on his face. "I told my friends, and they told their friends and their family, and eventually the whole town knew about the boy who froze, *literally*, when he was angry."

He sighed. "A week after that episode on the marina, a... *thing* came. We were playing a board game. It..."

He swallowed. "It knocked down the whole wall, streaming fog. The worst part was... *I was the only one who could see it.* No one else noticed the wall gone, no one else noticed the sudden fog, no one else saw that... *thing.* I escaped, but... that was it. It took my parents. I don't know what happened to my sisters. I never saw them again."

"I'm sorry," I said quietly. The air felt cold. Heavy.

"A man showed up, and he brought me to Fort Calmier. An Áccyn soldier."

"You told me your parents lived in Fort Calmier," Nick said slowly. Natanian shook his head. I looked away from him. I had no idea.

"The fire's dying down, Jack," Bancroft broke the silence. Natanian relaxed at the change of subject.

"It's Nick's fault," I said, a little too loudly.

"Hey!" Nick complained, a little too enthusiastically.

"You wanna spark it again?" I encouraged. He raised his hand and looked up at me. An orb of electricity appeared in his palm, a couple stray sparks racing up his arm. "I wish I could control it that easily," I said with envy.

"Oh, you will," Natanian encouraged. "As long as you don't die first." The heaviness in the air began to fade.

"Nice having a break from your Master?" Nick grinned.

Bancroft stood up, "Draw your sword, *Nicolas Krom.*" Nick groaned.

"You totally asked for that one, Nick." I grinned, laying back in the grass. Nick threw his orb of Lightning into the fire, which burst to life. He stood up. Natanian slammed his hand into the ground, and Ice shot out across the forest floor beneath Nick's feet, curving around the campfire. He flailed on the suddenly slippery ground and crashed to his back.

"Natanian!" he shouted, shoving himself to his feet. Natanian laughed. Bancroft lunged. Nick barely got out of the way in time.

"You dropped your guard," Bancroft chided.

An orb of Water shot past, inches from Nick's head, and exploded against a tree trunk, sending a shower of bark over us and extinguishing the campfire. We were plunged into darkness.

I leaped to my feet and spun around to see Daniel step out of the trees, Water twisting up his arms, over his sharp, red-on-black Ealdra uniform.

I drew my sword, "Oh, hey, I know you! You tried to kill us."

"They're coming, Nicolas," Daniel said quietly, "The Ealdra. And the Sheriff. *Traitor.*"

Nick raised his sword, and Lightning arced up his arms, flashing down the Damascus blade. His cold light splashed against the trees around us, lighting up Daniel's smiling face.

Daniel threw his arms down to his sides, and swirling orbs of Water formed in his hands. Natanian shouted, sending a blast of Ice hurling through the air at Daniel. Daniel threw up his arms, and the Ice hit his wave, crashing to his feet in puddles of slush. He spun, flinging a jet of Water at Nick. Nick slammed his sword into the earth, a blast of Lightning bursting up before him. It shot through the Water, evaporating it, and struck the trees.

The woods roared into flame.

Nick drew his sword from the ground and straightened up. Daniel stood his ground, looking between Natanian and me.

"You're *all* True Born," he realized. "Fun." He raised his arms and threw them out. A ring of Water exploded from him. I dropped to the ground. The Water sailed over my head, spraying my face with tiny droplets. The Water hit the burning trees around us, and they burst from their roots, crashing back into the dry forest floor. It all flared up around us.

Daniel drew his sword.

FOURTEEN

DARK SHADOWS JUMPED IN the burning trees. Dark forms, wielding shining blades in the blazing forest. And Daniel, twisting orbs of Water in his hands, flashing in the firelight. Nick stood beside me, Lightning crackling around him.

I felt a cold Wind blow through the clearing, whipping the flames into an inferno. Burning smoke flooded my throat. I coughed, raising my sleeve to shield my nose and mouth as more smoke was conjured by the rising wind.

"Look what you've done, Nicolas!" Daniel shouted, striding forward through the fire, steam rising around him. *"Look at yourself! Look around you!"*

Nick's hands tightened on his sword hilt. Something flickered behind his eyes, and he shut them tight. He took a deep breath, and when he opened them again, they shone with a strange light. His face was hard as stone. A bolt of Lightning crashed from the sky between them. I jumped back, my hair standing on end. Daniel landed back on the forest floor, grinned, and swung his arm around. Nick lunged away. The ball of Water, flickering with electricity, roared past his head and exploded into the forest floor, sending up a cloud of steam.

The shadows leaped out of the tree line. Two Ealdra soldiers were racing toward me. I gritted my teeth and raised my hand, focusing on the flaming debris falling around me. My Wind whirled up, holding the debris in midair. I flicked my wrist, and a shower of flaming leaves and sticks crashed into the Ealdra soldiers. They burst through the debris with hardly a second glance. One of them, lunged toward me, her face tightened with adrenaline, eyes wide with the excitement of battle. Her sword flashed up, the Damascus steel swirling red in the firelight.

I threw up my sword. *Too slow.* Searing pain slashed across my leg. I screamed. My leg buckled under me. Bancroft leaped forward and swung his sword in a wide arc. The two Ealdra soldiers fell back, the woman's blade shining red with my blood. Bancroft's weapon flashed. Another blast of Lightning crackled around us. I pushed myself to my feet, electricity and pain shooting through my body, stabbing my leg. I cried out and collapsed.

Bancroft grabbed me, pulling me back, his sword covering me. "Jackson, how bad is it?" Hot blood streamed through my fingers, brilliant red in the flickering flames.

My head spun. I looked away, "I..."

"Let me help you stand up." Bancroft reached down, and I threw my arm around his shoulders and heaved myself up.

My leg screamed in protest. I gritted my teeth, clenching my sword hilt. The world spun around me. I closed my eyes tight, and when I opened them, I saw Nick and Daniel on the other side of the clearing, Nick's clothes singed, as electric blue and fiery light danced around them. Two Ealdra soldiers lay dead at their feet, smoke curling from their clothes.

A loud *snap* rang through the air, and the trees groaned.

"*Look out!*" Bancroft shouted, shoving me away. I hit the ground rolling as a huge tree swung down through the air and crashed to the earth in a blaze of fire. Hot air blasted my face. New energy rushed into me. The searing pain in my leg gave way to the terror dancing through my mind.

I pushed myself to my feet, my jaw clenched tight, and grabbed my sword off the ground. An Ealdra soldier was sprinting across the clearing, straight toward Natanian. He didn't notice, his blade locked with another soldier's. I took off toward him, and with a shout of rage and raw fear, I swung my sword. The Ealdra soldier leaped back. He spun on me and lunged forward. I sidestepped, knocking his blade away. He slashed again. I twisted, throwing up my sword. Our blades hit with a ringing clash.

He drew back his foot and slammed it into my injured leg. I hit the ground on one knee, blood pounding in my thigh. The soldier stomped down on my blade. Cold steel slid against my neck. My breath caught in my throat.

I was going to die here.

It was all going to end here.

I felt a pulse of cold in my chest and the sudden roar of my North Wind. The soldier flew back, high into the trees. I collapsed to my side. Then Bancroft was there, grabbing my arm, pulling me to my feet. I swayed a second, waiting for the world to rush back into focus—the trees, groaning and crackling under the roaring flames, burning debris raining from the heavens, the ringing clash of steel, the blood on the ground.

My head cleared, and I snatched up my sword. An arrow whistled past my head. I jerked back in surprise and saw an Ealdra soldier on the other side of the clearing, merely a shape in the trees, pull back on a longbow for a second shot. Bancroft shoved me aside. A second arrow whizzed past us.

A tall, scruffy man stepped out of the trees, wielding a longsword. *The Sheriff.* A dozen Hunters emerged from the trees all around us.

Then Perry tore free from where he was tied and bounded up to me. I caught him, holding tight to his antlers as flames burst above us.

"Go!" Bancroft shouted.

I swung up on Perry's back and bent over his neck, "Stay low," I whispered. There was no way we were getting up through the canopy without getting shot.

Natanian slammed his hand into the ground, sending a rippling wave of Ice across the forest floor.

"Sheriff!" A Hunter shouted, pointing at me. The Sheriff spun around and drew his sword, striding toward me. Perry reared back and leaped over them. The Hunters slashed.

We hit the ground on the other side of them, and Perry launched again, tearing through the trees, streaking low as flames and sparks flashed around us. I heard the hum of an arrow. We dove over a small drop-off. The arrow thudded into the tree above our heads. We landed hard, and I slipped on the Peryton's soft furred back, nearly losing my balance. I caught my sword before it could drop, and bent low over Perry's neck. *The Hunters were here.*

We darted in and out of the trees, branches whipping past. I heard a dull whistle. I jerked Perry sideways, and he let out a high screech and banked too hard. I pitched forward over his head, crashing through brush and sticks. My feet flew out into dead air. My stomach dropped. I clawed at a rocky ledge as I passed, and caught hold of the very edge.

For a moment I hung there on the rim of the outcrop, the trees towering above me, flames flashing in the darkness. And poor Perry, his legs tangled in a grappling net, struggled helplessly as two Ealdra archers stepped out of the trees.

Then the ledge crumbled. I fell and fell, the rocky cliff vanishing up into the darkness. I hit the ground hard, the wind rushing out of my lungs. I crashed down a steep incline, tumbling across sharp stones and sticks that cut into me, finally coming to a stop flat on my back.

For a moment, I stared up through the trees at the stars above, gasping for breath through the smoke that hung in my lungs. The world tipped and spun around me.

I rolled over with a groan. The light of the fire was gone. All around me loomed dark trees and steep slopes. I pushed myself to my feet and started running up the nearest hillside. Blood pumped through my ears. My body was crying in pain, every step sending sharp stabs through me.

A cliff's edge loomed out of the shadows before me. I changed course and raced up the incline, pulling myself the last few feet up the ledge. The forest fire blazed before me. I staggered forward, shielding my nose and mouth, pain shooting through my injured leg. A scream rang through the air.

"*Nick!*" I shouted. My pain vanished with a fresh pulse of adrenaline. Ice-cold Wind whipped through the air. I sprinted up the next slope. The Wind blew faster and faster, twisting up the flames in a swirling torrent around me. The noise of battle had died out. The fighting had stopped.

A deadly silence had fallen across the forest, broken only by the crackle of the fire.

"*Nick!*" I shouted again into the blazing woods. There was no response. Still I ran, tearing past blackened trees, my cold Wind whipping at my face, bursting out from my hands wherever I brushed against branches. Something flashed on the ground in front of me. I slid to a stop. *Nick's sword, half-buried in the dirt.*

A second cry rose above the crackle of flames. I snatched up Nick's sword and took off through the trees. The ground turned slippery with water. Steam hissed around me.

"*Natanian!*" I yelled, spinning in a circle, trying to locate his cries. I crashed through the branches. "*Nick!*" I screamed. "*Bancroft!*" My voice echoed, seeming to mock me.

My leg gave out under me. I collapsed, panting on the ground. I looked down at Nick's sword. A trickle of blood streamed down the dark, Damascus steel. I felt light-headed. The world started to spin. *No, no, I couldn't pass out. There was no one here to help me. There was No. One. Here.* My pant leg was red with blood. Somewhere far away, another tree crashed to the earth.

There was nothing and no one here but the crackling, roaring fire, and the cold, biting Wind that I could *barely control.*

FIFTEEN

I JERKED THE MAKESHIFT bandage tight and tried to ignore the stab of pain. The forest fire was moving away now. I sheathed Nick's sword and grabbed a long stick that had somehow managed to escape the flames. I pushed myself up with a grunt, balancing on the crutch.

"Come on, Jack," I said to myself. I took a step. The crutch hit a stone and flew out from under me. I fell to my knees.

The ground was cold beneath my hands. Smoke filled my nose and mouth. Blood tingled against my tongue. My hands were shaking. I struggled to take hold of the stick again. *They were gone. They were all gone. The Ealdra and the Sheriff had taken my friends, and disappeared.*

I coughed, the smoke-filled air burning in my eyes and lungs. My Wind twisted the smoke around me. I breathed out, trying to take control of it. I couldn't grab hold, I couldn't bring it back to me. I had no idea where the Ealdra could have gone. I wasn't strong enough to go after them, let alone fight them. I was alone, lost in the smoking forest, *with no way to contact any help and no way to get to my friends.*

I sat back, looking up at smoldering trees towering around me, and coughed again. I looked down at my hands. Trembling. Covered in soot and dirt and blood. I was weak.

Everyone said I was the strongest they had ever seen, though. *Was I that person?* I had to be. *I am powerful enough to be hunted.* I grabbed hold of my makeshift crutch. *I am a descendant of Robin Hood. I am a descendant of Rowan Tyler.* I pushed myself up on one leg and braced the crutch under my arm, gripping the hilt of Nick's sword tight. *I am a True Born Rangerian. I am the Great Guardian of the North.*

No.

More.

Running.

In one heave, I pushed myself up, steadying myself on the crutch. *I had run for weeks. I was stronger than this.* I took a step forward, then another, and another, walking past the pain in my leg, bracing myself on the charred trunks of trees as I moved. I stopped trembling. The smoke began to fade around me. I was alone. If I was going to survive, I was going to have to face whatever and whoever was hunting me down.

And I would find my friends. No matter what it took.

I moved steadily through the forest, the smoke thinning the further I walked. Tendrils of cold, gray mist drifted down my arms. Light was creeping over the horizon, filtering through the trees. There wasn't anything burnt over here. The filtered sunlight instead fell on golden leaves, making the ground look like it was still on fire.

Then I saw something ahead, fallen in the undergrowth. I quickened my pace, hobbling up to a large oak. I bent down and shook Bancroft's sword belt free from the leaves. It was torn and singed, the buckle loose.

A branch snapped in the trees. I whipped around, staring through the haze. A shadow, the Dark Archer, flitted between the trees... and was gone. I could still feel her watching me. I swallowed my fear and drew Nick's sword.

"Who are you?" I shouted. My voice was hoarse. "Why are you following us?" I waited what seemed minutes for an answer, though it was probably only a few seconds. I wasn't sure what to do next.

Then a black-gloved hand gripped the tree trunk in front of me, and the Dark Archer stepped out. Thick smoke drifted between us. Dark, piercing eyes shone beneath a hood. Her deep green cloak swirled across the dry ground.

I took a step forward. The Dark Archer raised her longbow and drew it back with the faint creak of the string on wood, and held it, motionless. I edged away. The tip of her arrow shone in the morning light. The black feathers of the fletching rippled. I was frozen, my sword half-raised, staring through the smoke that grew by the moment at this Dark Archer who stood, unmoving.

Then the smoke swirled black, and the archer was gone.

I blinked, lowering Nick's sword. I couldn't remember when I had drawn it. The smoke cleared.

I gasped, staring up through the trees at towering turrets rising high above the branches, the sharp pinnacles stabbing into the golden sky. *How far had I come?*

Sixteen

I FELL BACK IN the tree line, breathing hard and fast. The red and black Ealdra flag fluttered over the battlements. I could see guards standing on the wall, scanning the forest below. Some were pointing off to the curling pillars of smoke behind me, rising from the smoldering trees leftover from the forest fire.

Nick, Natanian, Bancroft, and Perry were in this castle. Somewhere, in those halls and chambers swarming with Ealdra, my abducted friends were being held captive. If Daniel's reaction to seeing Nick indicated how the rest of the Ealdra would treat him... there was no way they would let him escape. Or let me break him out. Maybe this power of ours *was* a curse, as the Sorcerer who made the Golden Arrow intended.

The gates swung open with a creak that carried all the way down the slope. I backed further into the tree line, into the shadows. I landed on a stone and my injured leg throbbed. I bit my lip, stifling a cry, and peeked out around a tree trunk. A group of Ealdra soldiers marched out the gate, talking loudly. I caught only a few words, but one of those was *Nick.*

I carefully moved around the tree trunk, looking up at the battlements, and shivered. The castle was massive. If I could even get in, how would I ever find Nick and the others? I knew Fort Calmier, I'd grown up there. But this was totally different.

I glanced over my shoulder. The group of guards was gone. I looked back, trying to find a way I could possibly get inside. High on the wall, someone had propped their spear against the battlements. An idea started to come to me. I was fast... If my leg would cooperate, I just might be able to make it.

I raised my hand and closed my eyes, sinking back into my body, driving down the pain searing through my leg, focusing on nothing but my breath and the feeling of the cold energy twisting in my chest. I felt the chill rise, tingling outward to my fingertips. I opened my eyes, concentrating on the spear. Cold Wind rustled through the leaves above me. The spear shifted slightly. I took a deep breath, letting the world fall away. This was much heavier than any stick I had moved during my training with Bancroft. But I had to do it. *I had to move that stupid spear.*

I took another deep breath, pushing away any bit of fear still festering inside me. I forgot about the soldiers on the path behind me. I forgot about the sharp battlements towering above me. I forgot about my friends and Perry likely imprisoned in those walls. I breathed out.

The spear crashed to the stone.

The noise made me jump. An Ealdra soldier appeared over the battlements, picking up his fallen spear. Not good enough.

Stay focused, Jack. I turned away and braced myself against a tree trunk, my leg twinging in pain. I closed my eyes, and this time, I let the pain and fear crash over me.

They were probably dead. All of them. I was never going to see them again. I was going into this castle swarming with soldiers who wanted my power, who wanted me dead. I was going to die. They were about to find me.

I was going to die.

I raised my arms toward the canopy above me. A gale of Wind blasted through the trees, catching the leaves and tearing them from their branches, twisting up through the air.

I glanced back at the wall to see the soldier lean out over the battlements in confusion. Then he pulled back and called to the other guard.

They were going to find me. They were going to kill me. I was never going to see my mom or my dad again. I was never going to see my Great-Aunt Isabel again. I was never going to see Kara, or Nick, or Natanian again.

A tornado twisted in front of me, swirling mist rolling off my arms, Wind tearing through the trees. The guards turned toward the Wind whipping through the forest before me.

"Who's there?" the soldier shouted.

This was it. I dropped my crutch and spun around the tree trunk, taking off toward the Ealdra castle. I bent low, skirting the wall, toward a small door a few yards away. I yanked open the door and ducked inside.

SEVENTEEN

THE COURTYARD WAS SWARMING with life. Carts carrying stacks of weapons rumbled past. In one corner, Rangerians sparred in front of a Master. I glanced down at my clothes, at my dirty jeans and sweatshirt, suddenly thankful I'd changed out of my Áccyn tunic. About half of the soldiers here—those who weren't on duty today—were dressed about the same as me, though much less dirty. I hadn't showered in several days and smelled strongly of smoke. If the smell and dirt didn't give me away, there was one other thing that that would for sure.

I was a Rangerian. That was dead obvious to any of these soldiers. There weren't too many of us, so everyone knew who the Rangerians of the court were. I had seen that pretty clearly in Fort Calmier. Now here I was, fourteen years old, a brand new Rangerian with no control of his power, carrying a satchel with the notorious name *Rowan Tyler* stitched on the inside. I was covered in soot, with the smoke of the still-burning forest fire I *must* have come from rising high above the trees outside. I should have thought through this plan a *bit* more. I pressed against a wall, unsure of what to do next.

A hand clamped down on my shoulder. I stiffened. A chill raced down my spine. I slowly turned around, looking up into the face of a very tall, very slim man. A wide smile spread across his face. The bell rang for the changing of the guards. I took a step back. Then the bell rang again. And again.

The carts were quickly wheeled away into the keep, the people who weren't armed flooding in after them as the sound of the warning bell pealed through the courtyard. The remaining soldiers drew their weapons and rushed toward the walls, toward *me*.

Oops.

"Hello, Jackson," the man's silky voice sent shivers racing out to my hands. My leg throbbed painfully. His fingers curled around the strap of my satchel and jerked if off my shoulder.

I grabbed hold of it. "I think you're mistaken, sir, that's mine." He ripped it away from me, that smile never leaving his face. "Oh, you don't want that," I laughed nervously. "I just found it, sir... in the forest. I was out getting firewood for His Kingship and—"

"Rowan Tyler," he read, tracing the letters.

"Who, sirship?" I swallowed. Soldiers were rushing around me now. Reinforcements had come, sprinting up the stairs to the battlements. I'd lost my last chance. There was nowhere to run now. I could only stand here before this extremely tall creep of a man, my feet glued to the ground, my cold Wind swirling around me, cursing the fact that I couldn't bring it under control, as the clang of the warning bell echoed off the walls. *Why hadn't they arrested me yet?*

The man sneered. "Who are you?"

"Oh, I'm... Jerry. Jerry Nicolas." I cursed myself again. *Nicolas? Really?* I forced a grin, holding out my hand. "And you are...?"

He stared at me with his unnerving smile, his long fingers folded around my great-grandfather's satchel. *"Who... are... you?"* he repeated slowly, staring straight through my eyes. The Wind swirling around me felt painfully obvious. But with that skinny head of his, he must have been a bit low in the brains department.

"Give me my bag back," I croaked, then grimaced. I *was* going for something a bit more threatening.

His smile only spread wider. "What are you doing here? You don't belong here. Does it have anything to do with that bell, I wonder?" He tipped his head, looking back at the bell tower, rising above the keep.

I closed my hand around Nick's sword in my sheath. So... that bell wasn't for me? If it didn't go off because I snuck in, what happened? Who triggered it?

"I don't know," I answered. "Give me my bag back. Please. Sir. Lordship." This time the words came out clearly, but I still wished they were a bit more threatening. I held out my hand, and the Wind picked up. I quickly dropped my arm, rubbing my hands together, trying to keep the cold chill from escaping further.

The man stared down at his hands, at the satchel. Then his eyes slowly moved up and fixed on me. Still, his smile never wavered.

"Who are you, Wind Rangerian?" He said the words slowly, emphasizing every syllable. My stomach

clenched. His smile widened. "There's only one of you left." He dropped his voice, and a strange, tingling hush fell around us. "You're Jackson Marcrombie." I gulped. The noises around us sounded muffled, distorted, to my ears. But his voice was clear as crystal. "You know I have orders to turn you over to the Sheriff. *They all do.*" He gestured to the soldiers now pressed in around me.

A sinking feeling ran through me. These soldiers couldn't hear a word we were saying.

Sorcery. It had to be.

The sorcerer straightened up, and with my satchel still clasped firmly in his slim hand, he moved gracefully through the soldiers who parted before him without even a glance. I limped after him, wishing now I hadn't thrown away my crutch. He still had my satchel. And he might be able to lead me to where the others were.

The instant I stepped out of the main courtyard, I reached for my sword hilt.

The sorcerer raised his hand. "You may think them unaware. But any move against me, and these soldiers will turn on you." His silky voice hung in the air. I released my sword hilt, my hands shaking. The rushing Wind around me did nothing to ruffle his gelled-back hair, let alone pull the satchel from his grasp.

He raised his hand to a tapestry hanging on the wall of the corridor as he drifted past. "It's incredible what a single arrow can do." The tapestry showed the Golden Arrow hanging from a wide oak tree against a sea of stars, moonlight glinting off the shining feathers.

"Yeah, cool," I muttered. He turned down a set of stairs, his feet in their tall boots stepping so smoothly he seemed to glide away. The foggy remnants of sorcery curled in tendrils around his feet. I glanced back at the tapestry. *This couldn't be... him... could it? He remembered the Golden Arrow, he mentioned the curse Sorcerer Gisborne had placed on it a thousand years ago...* I swallowed. This had to be him. I didn't know how, but it had to be.

The Sorcerer.

With a capital *S*.

I shoved the thought away and jumped down the stairs after him. I wasn't going to leave my friends. If I kept playing along with this thousand-year-old Sorcerer, if he didn't eat my face, he might lead me right to them. And I wasn't going to lose Grandpa's satchel. He hadn't lost it in all his years as a Rangerian, and I wasn't about to now.

The staircase moved deeper and deeper into the castle, further and further underground, twisting through fog.

Eighteen

T HE DOOR SLAMMED INTO the wall. Silence fell in the long hall, ringing across the pillars. The Sorcerer strode across the black tile, the intricate columns rising and curving around the ceiling above him, the sunlight streaming through the windows turning to darkness as he passed.

"You had one job!" His voice resounded in the hall.

Androuet dropped to his knees. The tall Sheriff, once standing so strong, looked tiny, shriveling before this terrible force.

"You had three chances." The Sorcerer's voice was dangerous. "Fort Calmier. His safe house. *Last night in the woods!"*

"My Lord..." Androuet's voice trembled.

He tipped down through the air, darkness collecting around him. "He was a scared, wounded little rabbit, left all alone in the woods, *AND YOU LET HIM GET*

AWAY!" He threw out his hand. One of the Hunters rose, struggling, off the ground. He clenched his fist, and the Hunter imploded into black fog. Thunder rolled outside.

The Sorcerer crouched down in front of Androuet. The Hunters cowered behind their leader. *"Do you remember who you are answering to? Do you remember who I am?"*

"Y-yes, My Lord."

"Do you?" His dark eyes flashed. "I am your greatest dreams and your darkest nightmares. I can make you a king *or I can turn you to dust."* He straightened, "If you fail one more time, you will answer to *me. I* own *you. You* serve *me.* I can destroy you one piece at a time. I can tear away everything you have ever cared about. *Or you can bring me a fourteen-year-old Rangerian."*

Sheriff Androuet looked up. "But, he's strong."

"I know that!" he shouted. "Look at me!" He grabbed Androuet's armor, lifting him off the ground. "Are you afraid of me, Androuet?" The Sheriff nodded quickly. "You should be. *I* am the one who caused all of this. *Look at me.* I conquered death. Eight hundred years, and I am stronger than ever before. But what we are

doing... if you fail, if you fail to raise the Gold King..." He pulled the Hunter close, "*I am nothing compared to what* he *will do to you.*" He let go.

The Sheriff dropped to the ground and scrambled back.

"Orin!" the Darkness shouted.

The boy Rangerian stepped forward and dropped into a short bow, "My Lord."

"This is your last chance. I will not stay on the sidelines anymore, because, apparently, you and your Hunters cannot handle *ONE LITTLE BOY.*" Orin winced. "I will help you, but there is only so much I can do to make this work." He raised his hand. Orin looked up, fear flickering in his eyes. "*You understand that, don't you?*" Orin nodded. "I will take Jackson back to where all of this began. And you are going to be waiting for him."

Orin swallowed his fear. "Yes, My Lord."

The Sorcerer stepped back. Fog streamed off his shoulders, pooling at his feet.

Nineteen

"OVER EIGHT HUNDRED YEARS," the man whispered, his voice echoing eerily off the walls as fog streamed off his shoulders, pooling at his feet. "Eight hundred years, Jackson. It's been such a long time." This man couldn't possibly be *the* Sorcerer... could he? A weird chill prickled the back of my neck. "I remember that arrow, perfectly balanced, every angle sharp as glass, every facet reflecting the moonlight in a hundred rays."

"How bored were you to think up that little poem?" I muttered. *There was no way he could be* the *Sorcerer.*

A thick fog coated the foot of the staircase. I froze. His fingers reached into his robes and pulled out a single, golden key. I stared down at the fog, at the dark corridor, at the golden key in his hand... and decided it didn't matter *who* that satchel belonged to, *I was not going down there.* I would figure out a different way to get to my friends. I turned and started back up the steps, two at a time, limping hard on my injured leg. I heard the man turn around, felt his eyes on the back of my neck.

"Jack?" A voice... Aunt Isabel's voice in the corridor below. *"Jack, is that you?"*

I swallowed. My throat felt twice as small as usual. My Wind was whirling around me, ruffling my hair, whistling against the stone. I turned back around and slowly limped down the steps.

The Sorcerer had not stopped smiling.

"Do something, please? Frown?" I offered. He only watched as I sidled past him.

I stopped at the foot of the stairs, staring down at the thick fog—the same kind of thick fog that cloaked Fort Calmier, hiding it from normal eyes. The same fog that lingered wherever there were traces of sorcery.

"Jack?"

We never should have left Aunt Isabel alone. I knew this was going to happen. I knew the Sheriff was going to get to her. I swallowed again, painfully, and glanced up at the Sorcerer. "All these eight hundred years and you haven't found a gel that doesn't turn your hair to concrete?" I taunted. He turned away, drifting ahead of me, his robe sweeping through the fog. He wouldn't take the bait. "Okay, then."

Something shifted in the corner of my eye. I whipped around, staring into the darkness of the cell beside me. We were in the dungeons. There was nothing there. I must have imagined it. I took a deep breath, and kept walking.

The Sorcerer was gone.

"That's it, run away, coward," I whispered, wishing I could do just that.

"The Great Guardian of the North," the sorcerer's silky voice echoed through the corridor. I stared through the swirling fog and flickering torchlight, trying to find him. "One of the strongest Rangerians anyone has ever seen." One of? *So there was another like me?* I spun in a circle, my hand tight around Nick's sword hilt. "Why *you*, Jackson Marcrombie? What's so special about *you?*"

There he stood. His eyes pierced the darkness from the doorway of an open cell. My satchel was gone. He lifted the pictures of grandpa. "Great-grandson of Rowan Tyler. He was great... but you..." He looked past the photos straight into my eyes. "I feel so much potential in you, Jackson Marcrombie."

"Give me those pictures back." My voice rang through the corridor. "Come on. They're just old photos." He twisted his hand and they burst into fog. I lunged forward with a cry. He disappeared into the fog.

"Jack!" Aunt Isabel lunged against the cell bars.

I leapt to her side. "Aunt Isabel! Are you okay?" Her hair was streaked with blood and had fallen out of its braid. Her robe was dirty and torn.

"They came. *They came!*" She screamed, her eyes wide. And she melted into fog, streaming across my hands.

An echoing voice behind me. "Jack, help! Someone! Help!"

I spun around. Natanian was there, backing away towards me down the corridor, his face smudged with dirt and ash, his eyes wide with terror.

A dark shape crept out of another cell and came toward us. It looked like a man, folded over, moving on his hands and feet. Its skin was leathery, its muscles glowing faintly with a cold, pulsing light. It had no eyes. It bared its teeth, turning its head to face Natanian. Rough horns stabbed out from its skull that curved in toward each other, the dark red tips shining sharp. It smelled like smoke, and dust, and the rotting brine of the sea all rolled into one. It laughed, a rasping, ringing snort that chilled the blood in my veins. I raised my sleeve to cover my nose, my feet frozen to the ground. Its fingers spread wide across the stone as it crept closer and closer toward Natanian and me.

"Jack!" Natanian shouted. His voice cracked. "That's it! *That's what was in my house.*"

I gulped. I raised my sword, my hands trembling.

The monster charged.

Blackened, human teeth bared from its blank face. I dashed to one side. The thing hit the wall behind me and crashed through, stone crumbling around it in a cloud of dust.

Natanian scrambled away. "No! Bad!" he screamed.

"Natanian!" I held out my hand, my heart pounding in my chest. "We have to run!" The last few stones crumbled around the thing. I coughed in the cloud of dust.

"Jack," Natanian choked. *"Jack!"* He smacked my arm and pointed, shaking so hard he nearly fell over. I glanced down at my arm, an eerie shiver running through me as a wisp of fog trailed off my skin. His hand had gone right through me.

"What..." I mumbled

The thing burst free of the rubble, clouds of dust falling from its leathery skin. I started back. It raised up off its front legs to stand up before us, towering ten feet tall. It tilted its head and grimaced. Where its eyes should have been there was nothing but rough, pulsing skin. Darkness rolled off its shoulders, across its face, burning away before it touched the stone.

"I can feel you..." it rasped through its drifting cloak. *"Rangerians!"* Its head swung around until it stared at me... well... until its head faced me.

I raised my sword, trembling. "Go away," I ordered.

It laughed again, a sound that tore through it, reverberating to the ends of its twisted fingers.

And it leaped.

TWENTY

I HEARD A WEAK wheeze and opened my eyes, gasping for breath as cold fog pooled off me and drifted across the stone floor. The monster had burst apart when it hit me, just like Aunt Isabel. Natanian, too, was gone. I turned at the noise, and my insides convulsed.

"Perry!" I shouted. My Peryton was lying in one of the cells, an arrow deep in his side. I gasped, racing forward, "No, no, no...."

His eyes met mine, pleading, his antlers shaking with every breath. And his head fell back.

My mind was reeling. I didn't know what I was seeing. I reached through the bars. I couldn't get to him.

"No, *no*... Perry?" I whispered.

The walls seemed to be widening, leaving me in a gaping cavern. My Peryton's eyes stared up at me, glassy, unseeing. Heat was welling behind my eyes. I looked down at the arrow protruding from his side, his fur and feathers stained red. My fingers curled around the hilt of my sword. I felt eyes on the back of my head. Rage boiled inside me.

I leaped to my feet and drew my sword, spinning to slash through the Sorcerer, to *hurt* him. The tall, slim man morphed before me... and I stood facing Nicolas Krom.

I froze, my blade millimeters from his throat, panting, my mind spinning circles. Nick folded his hands behind his back and straightened up, his dark, mismatched eyes shining in the torchlight.

"Who are you?" I screamed through the twisting vortex of my mind.

Nick shook his head, "Have you not guessed yet?" I lowered my sword. He smiled, and took a step forward. Fog spilled off his shoulders, swirling down his arms.

"You're the Sorcerer," I breathed. "Guy of Gisborne." His smile widened. *Something behind his eyes...* I swallowed. *"You're not Nick!"* I swung my sword with all my might, screaming in the flood of rage.

Nick raised his hand, and a shockwave blasted into me. I flew into the air and slammed into the wall beside my dead Peryton. But Perry melted into fog that spilled across my legs and hot relief flooded my veins.

Nick stepped forward, "Are you sure I'm not Nick?" Lightning rekindled in his palms, the light flickering across his face.

"Jackson!" Bancroft slammed against the bars opposite me, sending a ringing clang down the corridor. Nick... no... *the Sorcerer* whipped around and shot a bolt of Lightning across the corridor. It hit the bars, arcing across the metal. Bancroft was blasted back and hit the opposite wall, his armor smoking.

I shouted, lunging forward. Nick spun back and threw up his hand. Another shockwave shot up in front of me. I bounced off and hit the ground, wheezing for breath. He took a step forward. Fog spilled over his outstretched fingers. I scrambled to my feet and raised his... *Nick's* sword.

"Stop!" I shouted. My head reeled. Nick... no. Stop it. It wasn't Nick. It wasn't. Nick was somewhere in these dungeons, locked in a dark cell. This was a sorcerer. *The* Sorcerer.

But what if he wasn't?

He took a step forward. I gripped my sword tight.

I was about to kill my best friend.

I felt the familiar cold chill race out from my heart, and icy Wind burst from my arms, racing down my sword as I shouted, leaping forward. Nick took a step back, startled for a moment. Then his eyes darkened, and he threw up his hand. Another shockwave slammed me back into the wall. I landed on the cell floor, gasping for air, my sword out of reach.

The Sorcerer stepped forward, his smile widening across his face. Electricity sparked in the whirling fog.

The *boom* of thunder rang through the corridor. The cell was filled with flickering light. Nick cried out and pitched forward to his knees. A second Nick stood behind him, Lightning sparking up his outstretched arms.

The Nick on the ground at my feet morphed back to the tall, slim sorcerer. I looked up at Nick, *the real Nick*, who was staring down at the man with an expression of half shock, half fear. Then he looked up and grinned. *Nick's smile.* One I knew well.

Nick straightened up. "You were about to run me through!" he accused, pointing a hand at the other Nick, flickering light filling his face. The Sorcerer backed off, scrambling across the stone.

"Come on, man!" I squeaked, my voice shaking slightly. "I had it handled." I spotted my satchel in the corner of the cell. I snatched it up and slung it over my shoulder.

"You're welcome." Nick stepped around the Sorcerer and clenched his fists. A low rumble of thunder sounded down the corridor. The Sorcerer didn't take his eyes off us, his gaze boring into us. His smile stretched wide across his face as he melted into fog. Nick cursed, dropping his hands.

"What... *who was that?*" I looked up at Nick.

"A sorcerer," he answered shortly.

"Not... *the* Sorcerer... the one from the stories. He said—"

"No," Nick interrupted. "Not *the* Sorcerer. Gisborne would not have let someone sneak up behind him." A wave of fog appeared around the corner, tumbling down the corridor toward us. "We need to move."

I slung my arm around Nick's shoulders and leaned into him. He clapped an arm around me. We ran down the corridor, the fog swirling around our feet.

"By the way, you made it!" Nick grinned. "You found us."

"Half of me made it," I corrected, wincing at the pain that shot up my leg. "Where are Natanian and Bancroft? Are they alive?"

"They are. Don't worry," Daniel's voice rang out. We slid to a stop.

He stood at the end of the corridor, flanked by six Ealdra soldiers. I groaned, "Not you again." I stepped away from Nick and raised my sword.

"The traitor prince is down here!" Daniel shouted. Six Rangerians came around the corner at the other end of the hall and began moving forward.

"This is what I'd call bad odds," I murmured, glancing around at Nick. Sparks flared down his arms.

The sorcerer appeared in front of us, his smile back on his face.

"Really?" I gritted my teeth and threw up my hand. Wind ruffled through his robes.

"Is that all you can do?" His silky voice drifted over the stone. Nick took a step toward him. Thunder rumbled down the corridor. The sorcerer's smile faltered. He threw up his hands, and Nick and I were separated by another shockwave. I landed hard on my bad leg and collapsed to the stone with a cry of pain. The cell bars slammed shut in front of me.

I scrambled to my feet. The sorcerer turned and drifted back down the corridor, past the Ealdra soldiers. In the cell opposite me, Nick pushed himself up and leaned against the bars, watching him go. There was a dangerous glint in his eyes. The air buzzed thick with electricity.

"Enjoy the stay, *Your Highness.*" Daniel swept a low bow, shot Nick a smirk, and strode back down the corridor, followed by his squad of soldiers.

"Traitor prince?" I said through my teeth clenched in pain. Nick stepped back from the bars and slid down the wall.

"Yeah..." he sighed. "Welcome to my father's castle."

Twenty-One

"STOP IT," COLTON SAID firmly, grabbing her hand.

Khadija leaned back and closed her eyes, taking a deep breath. She squeezed his hand tight. The air felt hot. But it always did around her. At least here, everything *else* was cold. Cold, and dank, and wet. "You are *not* what they say you are. You are *not* a monster."

"Then what am I?" The torch outside her cell flared, flame roaring up to the ceiling before dying back down to a small flicker.

"I'm not like you, Colton. I'm not a *good* person."

"Is that what *they* said?"

She dropped her head, pulling her legs up to her chest.

"No... maybe?"

"Who said it?"

"I'm down here, aren't I?"

"You're not a monster, Khadija."

"They call me the Dragon for a reason." She looked up at him through the iron bars of the cell. Her short, streaked hair reflected the black and red Ealdra colors. "Colton." Her eyes felt hot, her face wet. "I didn't mean for anyone to get hurt, *I promise.*"

"Hey." He turned around and reached through to grab her other hand, "I *know*. It's not your fault. It was an *accident*." He squeezed her hand. "You feel hot."

She laughed a little. "When am I not?" He smirked. She shook her head.

"Here." Colton moved closer.

She brushed her tears from her face. He closed his hand into a fist and ran it across the bars. Thin swirls of frost curled around the iron, twisting in patterns across the cell wall. She rested her hand against the stone, feeling the cold frost soothing on the back of her neck.

"Thank you," she murmured. She made herself relax completely. She breathed out, and raised her hand before her. The Breeze around her held steady, gently swirling around her hand. Then it caught the flame of the torch and spilled over, streaming through her control, the flame racing up the wall, roaring across the ceiling. She cursed.

Colton slammed his hand into the flaming wall and thick, white frost raced across the stone, extinguishing the fire.

"Do not lose your concentration," a voice said calmly from the cell beside hers.

"I *know!*" she screamed in frustration.

"Khadija."

She looked up. Two yellow eyes watched her from a crack in the stone.

"Lay down."

"I'm not doing that anymore!" she shouted.

The person paced away. But it wasn't a person. It was a panther, with the thin outlines of golden cheetah spots scattered across its back.

"Calm your energy, little Dragon. Let go of your power," the panther purred.

She laid back on the cold stone. They didn't call her 'the Dragon' because of her temper. They didn't call her that because of her skill in a fight. It was because she burned things. And her court hated and feared her for it.

Because she didn't just burn her clothes and her curtains. *Elena Bennet.* She closed her eyes against the grief and let herself melt into the floor. They were afraid of her. She was still so young for such strength. They called her the strongest Rangerian anyone had ever seen. They feared what she would become in the future. When she got out of this cell. When she mastered her power.

When she became queen.

She took a deep breath and spread her fingers across the stone.

"Tell me what you feel," the panther ordered.

"I feel the stone beneath me. I feel my heart on my ribs, my breath in my chest."

"Do you feel Colton's Frost?" Cold drifted across the stone toward her. She felt his Frost spread beneath her hands, curl around her fingers.

"Yes," she breathed.

"Focus, Khadija."

She let the floor, the Frost fall away, and she felt the energy in her chest. It was dry, electric, pulsing. The Masters said that North Wind was ice cold, South Wind hot; West Wind brought words, messages, whispers... but East Wind was pure energy, taking heat and cold and flame, and turning it up to eleven.

"Do not lose your concentration," the panther repeated.

Khadija let the energy in her chest seep out along her arms and gather in her palms. She felt the Frost on her fingers turn to cold mist.

"Now get rid of the Frost."

She stretched out her fingers, feeling the warmth in her veins. Then the Frost turned to ice and shot out across the floor and up the walls. She shouted in anger.

"Stop," the panther ordered. Khadija clenched her teeth, breathing fast and hard. "Try again."

"No!" She bolted to her feet and stumbled back into the wall. Flame roared up behind her, turning the ice to streaming water. *"It doesn't work, Daetho!"*

"You need patience," the panther answered calmly.

"How much longer?" she shouted.

"I don't know," he admitted.

"Maybe Rangerians weren't meant to learn control without their Tyrest. Whoever broke my vial can *burn!*" she cursed.

"Even with their Tyrest, Rangerians don't learn to contain their power for a while. And the True Borns, such as you, take even longer. Your court knows your strength, Khadija Krom. They will stand behind you. But if you do not learn to contain your power, your part in this coming war with the Áccyn will be more disastrous than any of us can imagine."

Twenty-Two

NICK SAT IN THE cell opposite me, twisting his titanium ring around and around his finger, the jagged silver Lightning bolt flashing in the torchlight. Low rumbles of thunder echoed down the corridor. The air felt heavy with electricity. I pushed myself up against the cell wall, wincing as pain shot down my injured leg.

I looked across at Nick. "What do we do now?"

The trembling fear in my stomach was growing stronger with each minute that passed. *They caught me. The Hunters were probably here now. Yes, I had stopped running... but because I'd lost.* My power was growing weaker by the hour, deep underground in this cell. And it would continue to weaken in the next few days, if I didn't get out. Then what would happen? If I stayed underground in these dungeons, if I didn't get outside, my power would continue to fade until it pulled me down with it.

I took a deep breath, closing my hand around my vial. *I wouldn't let that happen. I would get out.*

"Nick?" I called again. "You alive?" There was a long moment of silence in which I turned my Tyrest vial over and over in my hand, waiting for his response. I glanced around. I could barely make out his form in the corner of the cell.

"Do you know what the Ealdra do to deserters?" he finally asked, leaning forward into the light, swiping a tear from his face that looked... almost black? I shook the image away. Weird trick of the flickering torch light.

I laughed nervously to myself. "Well..." I tucked my Tyrest back in my shirt and turned to face him. "I've heard stories. They set the Sheriff or monsters after you. You're basically banned for life."

"It's a death penalty."

My stomach dropped. "Oh. Whoa."

"So if the crown prince deserts..." he tossed a stone up and caught it, laughing to himself. "By the way, you've taken that news surprisingly well."

"What, that you're royalty?" I paused. "I'll freak out on you when we *aren't* about to die," I promised.

"How's your leg? "

"Hurts like all high heaven."

"I don't think that's the expression."

"You can shut up, Your Highness."

"Think you can run?"

"What?"

He stood up. "Can you run?"

"Nick..." I pushed myself to my feet, "What are you saying?" He only stared at me, his smile spreading. "I'm not sure," I answered. "I ran from a sorcerer, so I guess so. But if you're planning on getting out, may I just ask *how*? On top of these iron bars, we're at least thirty or forty feet underground."

He stood up, "I'll get us out. Keep away from the bars," he advised. I took a step back.

Nick grabbed the bars around the lock of his cell, and Lightning burst across the iron, reflected behind his eyes. Flashes of electricity shot across the damp walls, crackling down the hall, into my cell. The iron beneath Nick's hands grew red hot. He let go, leaned back, and slammed his foot against the lock. It flew open, hitting the opposite wall with a resounding *clang* that echoed all the way down the corridor.

"Oh, okay." I grinned, the terror falling away. If we could figure a way out of these cells, we could surely figure a way past the guards. Or just melt them like those bars. He strode across the corridor and grabbed hold of the bars of my cell.

"You couldn't have done that earlier?" I complained. "We've been sitting here for *how long?*"

He eyed me. "You're going to need to bust these open once I get the lock loose." Lightning flashed across the iron, arcing up his arms. The bars turned red-hot in his grip. I moved forward and gritted my teeth, shifting my weight on my bad leg and slammed my other foot into the lock. It jarred, damp air steaming against the hot metal, but didn't give way.

I took a deep, shuddering breath. "Can't you melt it a little more?"

"Jack, I'm not going to get molten metal all over my hands."

"Fine." This was my one chance. I moved forward, leaned into my bad leg, and slammed my foot into the lock with every bit of force I could muster. I fell back, stifling my cry of pain. The lock swung free.

Nick moved forward and wrenched it open the rest of the way. He stepped inside and reached down. I grabbed his arm and he pulled me up. I slung my arm around his shoulders and drew my sword.

Shouts rang from the staircase as the guards realized what was happening.

"We have to move," Nick whispered. He dragged me forward, breaking into a run. My leg screamed with every step I took. We rounded the corner, torches flashing past.

"Is there another way out that's *not* up a forty-foot staircase?" I murmured.

"Nope. We just have to draw them away. Then circle back and... hope for the best?"

"That's your plan?" I shouted in a hoarse whisper. *"Hope for the best?"*

"Do you have a better one?" he snapped.

"Well, I'd think *you* could come up with a better one, seeing how you *grew up here!*"

"This *is* my better one."

I smacked him in the chest with my sword hand. "Shut up. There's Bancroft." We stopped in front of a dark cell. Master Bancroft recognized us and jumped up. He looked a little battered, but other than that, pretty much unharmed.

Nick unslung me and moved forward. "Stand back," he ordered. He pressed his hand to the lock, and the metal began to glow beneath his touch. Bancroft slammed into his cell bars, and they flew open. He caught the edge before it hit the stone.

"Nick? You okay?" Bancroft asked. Nick waved him off. "Jack, I thought I'd lost you," Bancroft whispered, crossing over to me as Nick strode up and down the hall, searching for the last cell he needed to bust open. "Are you okay?"

"Where's Natanian?" Nick demanded.

"They got him." He turned around. "They took him away."

"No…" I gasped through the pain.

"Guys," Nick warned. I looked up. Drifting fog appeared at the end of the corridor, rolling toward us. "We need to get out of here," Nick muttered. Bancroft slung my arm around his shoulders, taking Nick's place, and we took off down the corridor.

Twenty-Three

WE TURNED THE CORNER, and the sorcerer's fog pooled against the wall behind us. I could hear the Ealdra guards' pounding footsteps echo down the corridors. We rounded another corner.

"Almost there," Nick said. We were nearly to the staircase.

"Nick!" someone called out as we raced past.

I looked back over my shoulder, "There's someone there." Nick, Bancroft, and I all stopped and turned. A figure appeared out of the darkness of the cells.

"*Nick*," I called as my friend strode toward it, back down the corridor.

"*Khadija?*" He stopped in front of the cell. I pushed Bancroft off and limped down the corridor to see.

"Get me out." A girl's voice.

"Are you… sure about this? You know what happens." There was a long moment of silence.

"Yes," she insisted.

I stopped beside Nick. I saw a girl, her black hair cut short, streaked with red highlights. Bleached blonde was revealed underneath, woven through braids. She was small in stature... maybe just over five feet or so, and thin. She was younger than Nick, probably my age.

Nick melted through the lock, and she stumbled out. Her eyes flew between all of us and fear flash across her face. She threw her arms around Nick, holding him tight.

"What happened?" Nick whispered, wrapping his arms around her. He glanced up at us.

"Not now," she shook her head. She smiled up at him. "You can't imagine how good it is to see you."

"Did it happen? Your Manifestation?" She stepped away from him with a nod, that fear returning to her eyes.

"So, who are you, ma'am?" I demanded.

"She's my sister," Nick answered shortly. He held out his hand toward her. "You know you're giving up the throne by coming with me."

"I can't do this anymore." She clenched and unclenched her hands.

"So, you are the lost prince." Another voice echoed in the flickering torchlight. My eyes came around, and I stepped back in shock. A large, black panther stepped up to the bars, its yellow eyes glinting as it watched Nick.

Nick glanced at Khadija. She nodded. He stepped up to the panther's cell. "I'm not lost." He grabbed the bars and they began to glow red beneath the flickering sparks of lightning.

The panther looked up at him, his yellow eyes shining in Nick's light. "This is not your time. You do not belong here."

"What is an Azomien doing *here?*" Bancroft demanded. "How did they catch you?" The panther crouched back, and pounced on the cell bars. They crashed open. He landed, swishing his tail and blinking his bright eyes.

He bore the thin, golden outlines of cheetah spots scattered across his back. An odd chill ran down my arms. I never thought I'd see an Azomien. They were supposed to be myths, things you threw in a bedtime story to spice it up a little.

The *myth* suddenly froze, staring up at me. His eyes seemed to bore straight through me. "I am Daetho. What is your name?" he asked in a voice deep and smooth, startling me.

I swallowed, "Hi, cat, sir. I'm Jackson Marcrombie."

Daetho looked around at Khadija, then back to me. "I see great power in you, Jackson." His voice rang low.

"Um ... thanks."

A call sounded down the corridors, "*Find the traitor prince!*" an Ealdra soldier shouted. He sounded close. Too close. I caught Nick's eye. His face paled slightly.

"Nick?" Khadija asked, her voice trembling.

"Don't worry. I'll get us out. We're almost there."

Bancroft slung my arm around his shoulder and I steadied myself on my injured leg.

"Khadija," the panther called. He crouched down. She hesitated a moment, then swung up on his back, laying against his neck. We took off, sprinting down the halls.

The panther bounded alongside us. We reached the foot of the stairs and raced up. I gritted my teeth, forcing down the pain that shot up my leg with every jolting step.

Finally, Nick stopped at the top of the stairs and pressed his ear to a door.

"*Hurry up!*" I hissed, glancing over my shoulder down into the darkness. I could hear soldiers racing up the steps toward us.

Nick waved at me to shush. A moment later, he threw open the door and we rushed out of the dungeons. "This way!" he called quietly, hurrying down the long corridor.

The door to the dungeons slammed open behind us, and fog spilled out onto the stone. The sorcerer stepped out of the doorway, his cloak trailing through the fog. Nick whipped around and sent a blast of Lightning at him. It missed, ricocheting off the stone. The sorcerer stumbled. We tore around the corner.

The pain in my leg was gone. Adrenaline pounded through my system, my heart hammering against my chest. This was it.

"I can run!" I shouted. Bancroft let go. I staggered a step, then kept running. A group of Ealdra soldiers raced around the corner.

"This way!" Nick skidded around the corner.

We sprinted after him. I could feel my power beginning to grow stronger again. A gust of cold air raced down the corridor, rippling through my hair. The stale smell of dust clung to the ground.

Another group of soldiers appeared ahead, and Nick tore around the corner. I could smell fresh air now. He sprinted around another corner. We followed until he skidded to a sudden stop.

My heart dropped.

A group of Ealdra soldiers stood before us on the edge of the wall. Two of them held the ends of poles that were bound to a young man... Natanian. One man stood in the center of the legion, the tip of his sword pressed to Natanian's side. He wore a thick silver crown on his black hair.

"Natanian!" I gasped. He looked up at us, his eyes wide with terror. I could feel rage building in Nick beside me, the air growing heavy with electricity. I waved to the king. "Nice crown, Your Majesticity." A shiver of fear raced through me.

"We aren't going to let you get away that easily." The king's eyes were fixed on me. I braced myself and raised my sword, feeling the ice-cold energy spread out to my fingers, up my blade. I had no idea if I was about to be able to control it, *but I was not going to let Natanian die.*

I did a double-take. Two more soldiers held tight to ropes bound to Perry. *My Perry.* He looked fine. A bit bruised and scraped, but fine. Maybe we had a chance yet.

The king glanced at Nick, worry in his eyes. I grinned. He *should* be afraid. "Kneel," he commanded shakily. "Or we push him over the edge."

The soldiers pressed into the poles. Natanian staggered on the stone. His foot caught the edge of the battlements, and he slipped.

I lunged forward. Bancroft caught me in the chest, holding me back. Natanian swayed, his eyes growing wider. He regained his balance, perched precariously on the very edge of the wall. Ice crept down the poles held by the soldiers.

"*Father.*" Nick took a step forward. His voice was dangerously low.

"Stop," the king ordered, his voice ringing across the wall. More soldiers moved forward, raising their swords. Nick clenched his hands, and Lightning

161

flickered up his arms. The soldiers froze. "What are you doing, Nicolas?"

"You forced my hand, *Father.*" He forced the last word out. The king shook his head, and I noticed with a shock how much Nick resembled him. *The same jawline. The same hair. The same long fingers.*

"Too long." The king raised his voice, his eyes moving back to me. "Too long you have evaded us, Jackson. We won't wait any longer."

Nick suddenly lurched forward, seizing one of the soldiers' swords. The soldier staggered back in surprise. Nick raised the blade, crackling with electricity.

"Jack, when they make a break for us, *run,*" he whispered. "There's a way out to the right. Down the stairs, through the door beside the bakery. I'll free your Peryton."

I gripped my sword tight, "What about you?"

"I'll be right behind you. Trust me." There was a strange note in his voice.

"Take them!" The king shouted.

The soldiers surged forward.

I took one last look at Natanian and spun on my heel.

TWENTY-FOUR

I SPRINTED DOWN THE last few yards to the stairs, with Khadija, the Azomien, and Bancroft right behind me. A deafening clap of thunder echoed across the stone, ringing in my ears. Bancroft let out a loud whistle for our Perytons. Up ahead I saw the bakery Nick had mentioned. And beside it, the door out. The guard drew his sword. Without warning, Bancroft swung, knocking him down.

I burst through the door. A scream rang out.

Natanian had toppled off the wall and was falling through the air. Perry dove from the walls, soared, and then tucked his wings, aiming straight for Natanian.

Lighting slashed the sky. High, terrible screams ripped the air.

"Nick said he'd be right behind us!" I shouted helplessly to Bancroft over the screams.

"Don't worry about my brother!" Khadija called.

Then Bancroft's Peryton appeared above the tree line, soaring towards us.

Bancroft grabbed Khadija's arm, "Can you get another Peryton?" She nodded and pulled free of his grip, slid off the Azomien's back, and swung up on Bancroft's Peryton. She held her hand down to me. I grabbed hold, and swung up behind her, and we launched into the air.

Shouts rang out. Archers flocked to the walls. We arced high over the castle. I saw Nick below, his sword drawn, the air around him burning with electricity. Soldiers lay dead at his feet. He wielded his blade as if he had been doing it for a thousand years.

"Hold on!" Khadija shouted. We rode a downdraft. Cold air rushed past us, the Peryton's wings beating in my ears. The stables flashed past in the other courtyard. There would be more Perytons there.

"Khadija, we just passed the stables!" I yelled over the wind. She ignored me, diving down. We landed in a long hall, intricate pillars rising and curving up the ceiling high above us, sunlight streaming between them. "Colton!" Khadija yelled, sliding to the ground and breaking into a run. There was a boy, probably a year older than me, with kinky curly hair, wearing a sharp Ealdra uniform. He stood looking through the pillars at the Lightning battle raging on the outer wall. He turned at the sound of Khadija's voice.

"Khadija! How did you..." He ran up to her and grabbed her into a hug, holding her tight.

"It was Nick. My brother broke me out." She glanced back at me. Colton's eyes flashed over my dirty clothes, and he took a step back. "No, no, Khadija..." He let go of her, backing away. "Your brother deserted." Colton nodded at me. *"He's* Áccyn."

I rolled my eyes, "Really, buddy? You haven't even met me yet! Maybe I'm awesome. Also, probably hurry it up, Khadija!"

"I'm leaving," Khadija told him firmly. Colton opened his mouth, but she cut him off. "I know what that means. Are you coming?" He looked up at me. I raised my eyebrows, waving at them to hurry it up. An electric *boom* echoed through the hall. I glanced nervously up at the outer wall.

"Yeah." Colton nodded. "I'm coming."

"Jack, go! We'll grab our Perytons and follow you." Khadija and Colton took off down the hallway, headed back toward the stables.

"Alright, just you and me." I spun Bancroft's Peyton around, and we shot out through the pillars into the open air.

Nick was slashing through the lines of soldiers a ways off. Lightning cracked around him. His sword flashed. Soldier after soldier fell at his feet. *Nicolas Krom. True Born Rangerian of Lightning. The Traitor Ealdra Prince.*

Khadija and Colton shot out of the courtyard below. I banked hard, soaring out toward the walls.

"Nick!" I shouted. Nick didn't seem to hear me. He threw out his hand, sending a bolt of Lightning into the last soldier's chest. Now he stood alone before his father.

The king raised his sword, glinting with gold. Even from here, I could see the paleness of his face. He was scared. *Terrified.*

"Nick, leave him!" Khadija screamed, banking below me on a golden brown Peryton followed closely by Colton.

Nick took a step forward. Lightning arced up his arms. I took a deep breath. *I was not going to leave my best friend.*

I dove. Wind whipped at my face as I plummeted for the castle walls. I shot past Khadija. I pulled up right above the walls, the Peryton hovering in the air.

"Nick!" I shouted, "Grab my hand!" He only stood there, his hands clenched, Lightning sparking up the Damascus blade he held, the metallic burning smell rising up around him. *"Nick, come on!"* I screamed.

The king suddenly lunged, raising his sword to strike down his son. Nick met my gaze, and grabbed my arm. The Peryton veered away. The king's blade slashed through empty air as we arced up and left him behind.

I saw another wave of archers sprint up the stairs. I held tight to Nick's arm as we soared out over the forest. Colton and Khadija launched from the trees below, the Azomien settling behind the Ealdra princess. Bancroft and Natanian fell in below us, riding Perry.

"Go!" Bancroft shouted. Nick didn't look back as we took off into the sky. I let go of him, sure now he wouldn't do anything drastic. He sat perfectly steady behind me, his hands gripping my sword belt. The air was heavy with electricity. Beneath us, a flock of arrows was launched from the battlements, falling short.

The smoke from the burning forest rose high in the morning sky, the glow of the flames still visible in the distance. A low rumble of thunder sounded overhead, and still we flew on, away from the fire.

Away from the palace.

Away from the king.

TWENTY-FIVE

COLD WATER SPLASHED ACROSS my face. I lowered my hands and sat down on the bank of the river, undoing the makeshift bandage on my leg. The heavy electricity lingering in the air around Nick had faded. It was incredible how much power could reside in one Rangerian.

I shut my eyes tight. I could still hear the shattering cracks of Lightning, the screams ringing across the battlements, the dull rumble of thunder in the air.

I winced in pain as I pulled the bandage around my leg free. I couldn't believe it only took two years, give or take, for most Rangerians to fully control their power. I wasn't surprised it had taken Nick longer than that. I had seen what he could do, I could still feel the tingling electricity from when he had lost control in his rage.

Bancroft sat down next to me and held out his hand. I gave him the bandage and sat back. He pulled apart the tear in my jeans to see the injury.

"It's a sword slash, right?" he asked. I inhaled sharply and nodded as he pressed his fingers to my leg. "It's not too deep. I can bandage you up so you can walk on it." I nodded again, breathing out. He left to find the first-aid kit Aunt Isabel had given us.

I saw Nick sitting back against a tree, talking with his sister and Natanian. I couldn't imagine what it must have been like for Nick, leaving all that behind just as his power manifested. He hadn't seen his sister in two years. Why did he leave in the first place? He had so much there... a family, a *throne*.

"I'm sorry." Nick looked up as Bancroft walked past, carrying the bag of bandages. "It's my fault Daniel came after us."

"It's not your fault." Bancroft, returning, stopped beside me and knelt in the grass. "He's hell-bent on taking you down. You did what you had to... leaving the Ealdra."

"So..." I sucked in a breath of pain as Bancroft began cleaning my wound. "When were you planning to tell us you're royalty?"

Nick pushed himself to his feet. "I'm not anymore. I'm a traitor. Didn't you hear them?"

"Well, I don't know whether to believe you on that *reversal of royalty,*" Natanian said. "I distinctly heard them call you the '*traitor PRINCE.*'"

Nick didn't reply.

"That was your dad's castle," Apprehension twisted up into my throat. I glanced at Bancroft as a crawling feeling settled in my stomach. "Um... Did..." I swallowed, looking back at Nick. "Did we end up in that forest on purpose, Nick?"

Nick shook his head, "I didn't want to go anywhere near it. But... we had to land. Just coincidence, I guess."

"Then how did Daniel find us?"

"What are you saying?" Nick leaned forward, his eyes dark.

"The spy," Bancroft answered, glancing up at me. He began to wrap fresh bandages around my leg. "There is no other way the Ealdra could have known about us.

The only ones who knew where we were, were your Great-Aunt Isabel and those at Fort Calmier."

"*Jackson*," Nick murmured.

"I'm sorry," I shook my head. "It's just the pain talking."

"How's this?" Bancroft looked up at me.

"That's great," I nodded. He pulled the bandage tight. "Ouch," I gasped, jerking away, "That's less great."

I glanced back at Nick. Something was not sitting quite right with me. And I hated it. Nick and I were best friends. I shouldn't doubt him. But... the way the sorcerer and the Ealdra talked to him and acted around him... it was like they were afraid of him. And maybe it *was* all because of the strength of his power.

But I had a feeling there was something else... something more.

TWENTY-SIX

I STRODE THROUGH THE trees, pushing branches aside. Cold Wind drifted around me. *The sorcerer, bending down through the air. Fog swirling across the dungeon floor.* I landed hard on a stone and gasped at the jolt of pain through my injured leg. I hopped over the stone and started down a short incline.

Natanian, held at the very edge of the battlements. The sound of iron bars slamming shut on me. Cold, so cold. I stopped at the bottom of the incline, where the ground dropped off into sharp cliffs that plummeted a hundred feet to the river bed below. *Diving on Perry, Nick's life slipping through my fingers. The look in his eyes... a thousand years of rage. The crackle of his Lightning masking the screams.*

I sat down on the edge of the cliff and dangled my feet over the edge, breathing in deeply. The wind up here was cold, blustery. I took another deep breath, and the images flashing through my mind fell away.

The sorcerer had seemed to know who my great-grandfather was. He seemed to think there was a connection between the Golden Arrow and Grandpa Tyler. *What was that connection?* Why did everyone seem to know who he was?

He was the True Born Rangerian of the North Wind. But that couldn't be all. Not with everything going on, not with the way that sorcerer reacted when he found my satchel. So what did he have to do with the Golden Arrow?

The Golden Arrow. That one thing that made us who we were, the one thing that had started it all. Maybe the Arrow had to do with the Sheriff's mission right now. Maybe Orin, me, and the other two Winds out there had something to do with it.

Aunt Isabel lunging against the bars, her hair tangled and streaked with blood. The pure terror in Natanian's eyes, the rasping laugh of that thing.

I gripped the edge of the cliff hard, forcing the images out of my mind.

"Jackson." The Azomien stepped off the incline and sat down next to me, bringing me back to the present.

I swallowed. "Hi, sir." I inched away. This Daetho cat scared me.

"How's your injury?"

I glanced down at my leg, "It's fine, sir."

His whiskers twitched as he looked out over the cliffside, wind rippling his fur.

"Is that all?" I swallowed. "I don't think someone like you, sir, would come after me just to ask how my leg was doing." I laughed nervously. A shiver chased down my spine. "I'm sorry, si- I mean I'm..." I swallowed. "I... I also don't actually know what you are," I said, changing the subject. "I mean I know *what* you are—you're an Azomien—I just... don't know who..." I swallowed again, *"who* you are." I looked away from him and cleared my throat, squinting into the sun.

His head swung around, those piercing yellow eyes staring straight through me.

"You don't have to keep calling me *sir,* Jackson." The panther lay down. "My name is Daetho. I am chief of the Azomien."

"You're—what, now? You're *chief* of... Is it true? All the stories about the Azomien?" The anxiety in my stomach turned to excitement.

A note of mirth crept into his voice. "Are *all* the stories ever true?"

"Well, I just..." I cleared my throat again. "Well, can you really... read my mind? Or leap a hundred feet in one jump?"

He laughed, a sound that reverberated deep in his throat. "The Azomien aren't superheroes, Jackson. We are guardians."

"Sorry."

"Lake Cloudia is a safe house, built to stand against the Sorcerer."

"Capital *S*," I interrupted.

He glanced at me, "Yes. Sorcerer Guy of Gisborne. We watch over your world."

"Oh."

"That is why I'm here. I am growing fond of you, Jackson." I didn't know how to answer. "I would not have left Lake Cloudia," he continued, ignoring my silence, "but news has been growing of a Rangerian much more powerful than has been seen for a thousand years. I thought it was Khadija, but then I saw you. *Two* Rangerians of such strength. I want to take you and Khadija to Lake Cloudia. Yours are not the only whispers on the wind."

"What do you mean?"

"It's true, Jackson. He is real and still very alive. Sorcerer Gisborne. I fear what he's seeking with this sudden rise in conflict between the Áccyn and Ealdra nations."

A chill raced down my spine. "Where *is* Lake Cloudia?"

"That I can't tell you. I can only show you, if you agree."

"What am I agreeing to?"

"You will leave your court and you will come to Lake Cloudia. I will train you in your power myself."

I hesitated. "I already have a Master."

"If what your friends say is true, you've already had two Masters."

I looked down at my feet. I still saw him in my nightmares. *Kane lying against the platform.*

"And what about my family? My parents, my aunt?"

"It will have to be put to the Council. We don't let just anyone into Lake Cloudia."

"I don't know." I waved back in the direction of the campsite. "I still have all of them."

"Think on it." He stood up. "You're being hunted. They *will* catch up to you. Forces are rising, Jackson. How long are you willing to wait?"

TWENTY-SEVEN

I STEPPED OUT OF the trees, back into the small clearing where Bancroft had set up camp. Natanian appeared through the trees carrying an armful of firewood. I saw Khadija sitting still beside the fire, watching the sparks drift up into the night sky.

I sat down across from her. "I don't believe we've been properly introduced. Hi! I'm Jack. North Wind."

"You're North Wind?" Her mismatched eyes widened. "Hi," she replied hesitantly. "My name's Khadija. I'm Rangerian of the East Wind."

Natanian dropped his armful of firewood on the pile. "You're East Wind?" he repeated.

"If you're East... that means the Sheriff only has half of us now." I glanced at Natanian as he sat down. *My odds of escaping just went up.* I might not have to go to Lake Cloudia after all.

"The Sheriff?" Khadija asked.

"Hired by the Ealdra, I think," I explained. "They're after the four Wind Rangerians for our power. That must be why your court locked you up."

"That's not why I was locked up." She was on her feet, pacing. Sparks flashed up from the campfire every time she passed it. "I can't control it!" she cried in frustration. The fire flared, exploding in a shower of sparks. I threw up my arms to block my face. The sparks extinguished against my sudden shield of cold Wind. Khadija was shouting now. "I've only had it for a few months. My vial is shattered, so I can't even *begin* to control it. I *burn* things. That's why they locked me up." The fire burned hotter and hotter, the coals glowing white-hot. She stopped, and dropped her hands to her sides with a sigh.

I grabbed Natanian's arm and dropped away just as the coals exploded. The ring of fire shot overhead and hit the trees, which burst into flames. The inferno roared against the woods, sparks rising into the air to mingle with the evening stars. I gasped, grabbing my injured leg as pain shot through my thigh. *The clash of battle roaring in my ears, Lightning slashing the air, dark shapes rushing through the trees toward me.*

"Jack!" Natanian grabbed my shoulder.

I shook the images from my head. Nearby, the Ealdra boy—Colton—had his hand pressed to the ground, and a sheet of thick, white Frost covered everything around us, extinguishing the burning trees. My breath puffed in thin clouds before me. The small campfire crackled warmly in the center of the clearing, no longer a roaring monster. Colton shot to his feet and ran over, catching Khadija as she sank to the ground. I looked around at Natanian. He was staring at the Frost, at the Rangerian who'd made it. He raised his own hand, and swirls of Frost curled across his palm. Khadija sank to her knees, Colton's arms tight around her.

"North is ice," she whispered, looking away from her trembling hands up at me. "South is fire. West carries words, whispers, and messages. But East Wind twists it all. Any bit of energy around me roars up stronger than it ever could."

The cold energy in my chest was buzzing, straining to get out. I took a step forward and breathed out, the energy settling back. Khadija's hand touched the Frost-covered ground, and energy shot from her fingers, turning the Frost to shining ice, the world frozen around us.

Natanian raised his hand, shining spirals of Ice twisting up his arm. Colton's eyes grew wide, his lips parted in awe at Natanian's True Born power. Then fear flashed across his face. The Ice suddenly detonated into massive shards.

I dove again for the ground. The shards shot overhead, impaling the trees around us.

"Khadija!" Daetho bounded from the forest, Bancroft sprinting behind the panther. They stopped on the edge of the clearing.

"I'm fine," Khadija whispered, hugging her knees to her chest.

"Jackson..." Bancroft looked around, moving toward me. "Do you know where Nicolas is?"

"I don't know," I answered, pushing myself off the ground, my heart racing as I brushed Ice crystals from my pants. "Haven't seen him for a while."

Natanian shook his head.

Bancroft stepped forward, "I just got this." He took another glance at Khadija, at Daetho sitting beside her in the middle of all the shining ice, and held out a small slip of paper. I took it hesitantly.

RETURN TO FORT CALMIER IMMEDIATELY.

WE ARE UNDER ATTACK.

THE SORCERER IS HERE.

My stomach dropped. I looked up. "But the Ealdra already have control."

"Sorcerer Gisborne?" Khadija breathed, reading over my shoulder. "He's got to be about eight-hundred years old now."

"The Ealdra have the throne. They do not have full control," Bancroft corrected. "There were rumors, that appear to be true. Sorcerer Gisborne is alive. He is finishing what the Ealdra started."

"What's going on?" Nick emerged from the tree line. I silently held out the paper. He took one look at it. "What's the call?"

I closed my hand around my sword hilt. "I'm going," I answered simply.

I looked at Natanian. A hungry light shone on his face as he stared up at the destruction around him. I grabbed my satchel off the ground and whistled for Perry.

Daetho raced over to me, "Jackson, if *Sorcerer Gisborne* is there—"

"He's not going to care about my parents. Or Kara. I'm not leaving them there. And then there's our oath, right?" I swung up on Perry, looking pointedly at Nick.

"Jack, they're the ones who are hunting you," Bancroft protested.

"To give my strength to Fort Calmier and the defenseless," I recited.

"I'm with you." Nick swung up on Bancroft's Peryton and addressed his Master. "We abandoned them once. That is our *home.*"

Bancroft didn't move.

"You are injured, Jackson," Daetho argued. "Natanian was just held as a hostage. How well are you going to be able to fight?" I looked around at Natanian, another cold chill racing through me as I watched the dark light behind his eyes. He turned to face us. And he nodded.

"We can do it. I know my power," I assured Daetho.

"You aren't going to abandon *us,*" Colton threatened.

"Then come with us." Natanian urged, swinging up behind me.

Colton raised his eyebrows and gestured at his red and black Ealdra uniform. "Remind me who you're fighting, again?"

"If you take me into battle I will burn the whole thing down," Khadija whispered, terrified.

"I don't believe that." Nick shook his head. "And *you* aren't in uniform. You've been locked up for... how long? The Áccyn didn't know who you *were*, and you've deserted already. You left your old self behind." He smiled mischievously. "Time to show them who you are."

A small smile spread across Khadija's face—the same smile Nick wore. She mounted her Peryton, and Daetho bounded up behind her. Colton threw up his hands in defeat and climbed up on his Peryton.

Nick held out his hand, "Master Bancroft?"

Bancroft nodded, "To Fort Calmier."

I leaned forward and patted Perry's neck. "To Fort Calmier." And we launched through the trees.

Twenty-Eight

W E WERE SPIRALING DOWN through the sky. The night was dark, only faint light shining from the stars above. Those stars faded as we descended through thick fog. There was always a thin haze around Fort Calmier, remnants of the sorcery used to hide it, but fog this thick... What could it mean?

We landed suddenly on stone. I couldn't tell which part of Fort Calmier we were in. The air was dead silent. I slid off Perry, landing as quietly as I could on the stone with my bad leg. I slowly drew my sword. A cold wind whispered through the air, stirring up the fog. My footsteps sounded muffled, the noise deadened in the damp air. I moved forward, staring through the twisting fog. I could barely see ten feet in front of me. The dark, hazy outline of stone walls rose before us. The Wind gusted as my heartbeat quickened.

"Jackson," Bancroft whispered. I breathed out, calming my Wind.

"We got a distress call, but I don't see anyone," Natanian said in a low voice. "Are you sure we're in the right place?"

For a moment, the fog parted, and I saw a familiar platform in front of rows of benches... or what used to be a platform. We were standing in the courtyard where my Manifestation ceremony had taken place. The raised stage had snapped in half and was covered in rubble.

I turned in a circle. A path had been torn through the benches, as if by a tornado. The boards had been ripped up, shattered, and hurled across the courtyard.

I swallowed. "Yes, we're in the right place."

"With me," Bancroft gestured at us, and began moving silently through the fog as it closed up again.

"HELLO?" Natanian shouted.

I jumped at the sudden noise. Bancroft hushed him. "Sorry."

"Gees, you're going to wake up the troll that lives under the castle," I murmured.

"There's a troll...?" Khadija began.

"Yes ma'am! Ten feet tall and purple," I whispered, trying to smooth over my fear. "On a slightly related note, is there any way these ruins are a sorcerer's illusion?"

"No illusion," Daetho shook his head. "This fog is the remnant of very strong sorcery, but no, no illusions are at work now."

"They *did* say a sorcerer was here," Natanian whispered.

"No, not *a* sorcerer." Bancroft shook his head. "They said it was *the* Sorcerer."

"This fog could not have been caused by common sorcery," Daetho agreed.

"Why did I come?" Colton muttered to himself. "This was a bad idea."

"You already deserted," Nick encouraged him, moving forward.

"Oh. Thanks." Colton scowled at him.

I climbed up on a pile of rubble. I saw something, on the very edge of my vision, moving in and out of view with the drifting fog.

"A staircase," I called quietly. "That way." We moved forward, winding through the rubble and up the steps.

The stones beneath my feet were cracked, and slightly slippery with the damp fog.

"I don't remember exposed staircases in Fort Calmier," Natanian whispered.

"Yeah, me neither." The fear in my stomach was growing by the second. Still there was no sound from the palace around us. It felt dead here.

We emerged at the top of the staircase. Fog swirled around us, so thick a swing of my blade could separate it for a moment. We were in the corridor above, with wide windows to my right overlooking the courtyard. The corridor was barely recognizable, the roof blown off most of the way, and the windows now nothing more than gaping holes. I heard a stone drop behind me, a footstep echoing across the ruins.

I spun around.

"What is it?" Nick asked. I stared back down the staircase.

"There's someone there," I whispered.

"Keep moving," Nick urged. I turned around and followed Bancroft on down the hall, glancing back occasionally. I heard footsteps again, ahead and below us. We all froze.

"You heard it that time, right?" I whispered.

"WHO'S THERE?" Bancroft shouted.

"What happened to *shush?*" Natanian chided in a hoarse whisper.

"Come out of the fog," Bancroft ordered, moving to look down into the courtyard below. Nothing happened.

"Let us continue," Daetho whispered, and padded ahead of us. We followed him silently.

I stared through the fog, trying to see who or *what* was here with us. I touched my thigh gingerly. My leg was beginning to ache from maneuvering around all the debris.

"Where *is* everyone?" Nick whispered. His voice hung in the air, his words the thing every one of us feared, but none dared to mention.

They were all gone, Áccyn and Ealdra. *Dead? Or taken?* And we were too late.

Ahead of us, where the hall should have stopped to split off into the castle, the wall was blown out into the air beyond. Rubble had piled up beneath it. I crept up to the opening. Dark shapes rose out of the fog.

It wasn't just the ceremonial courtyard, or this corridor. I saw cracked, broken walls, collapsed towers, and splintered wood spanning what had once been my home.

Nick raised his hand, and a sparking orb of Lightning ignited in his palm. The flickering light fell on the stone around us. Some of the bricks were scorched black.

"How did this happen?" My heart was racing. Everything was gone. What happened to my parents? To Kara? I should have brought them all with me when I escaped.

"*Nick*," Khadija gasped, pointing.

There stood the Dark Archer in the courtyard below, an arrow nocked on her bow, moving through the swirling fog toward the pile of rubble that stretched down before us.

TWENTY-NINE

NICK STEPPED FORWARD AND raised his sword, crackling with Lightning.

"Who are you?" he shouted. The Dark Archer spun, her arrow whistling through the air. Nick jerked back. Before it hit the stone, the archer had another arrow on the string. In that brief moment, Nick dove forward, sliding down the pile of debris toward her.

"Nick!" I shouted after him. "Well, here we go." I scrambled down the pile into the fog.

"Jack, stop!" Bancroft grabbed at me and I slipped out of his grasp.

The archer didn't move, standing in the shifting fog only a few yards away.

I stepped off the pile of rubble and raised my sword before me. She silently moved forward through the fog and turned, slowly, away from Nick until her arrow was pointed right at my chest. I took a step back.

"Where is it?" she demanded.

"I don't..." I started to answer. The others scrambled down after me to the courtyard floor.

The archer took a step forward and drew back her bow. *"Where is it, Jackson?"*

"Whoa," I backed up, raising my sword in defense.

"I first thought it was in this castle, but I was wrong. *Where is it?"* Bancroft moved forward. The archer spun on him and let an arrow fly. Bancroft ducked away and the shaft shot past. When she faced me again, another arrow was on the string. "I'm only really interested in you, Jackson."

"What—?"

A blast of Ice shot over my head. The archer let her arrow loose and threw up her hand. A wall of darkness shot up in front of her. The Ice shattered into a million shards.

"Shadow," Bancroft gasped.

"You're a Rangerian!" I took a step forward, trying to see beneath her hood.

She drew back another arrow pointing at my chest. *"Where is it?"* she hissed.

"I don't know what you're talking about."

Now she was only a few feet from me, with the deadly weapon aimed at my heart. "Was your great-grandfather Rowan Tyler?"

"Yes."

"Rangerian of the North Wind?"

"Yes!"

"Then stop playing with me! Where is it?"

"Where's what?" My heart was pounding in my throat. The arrow flew from her bow, whistled past me, and sank into a crack in the stone, an inch from my head.

Bancroft had crept up behind her, and his sword slipped against her throat. She froze.

"Lower the bow," he whispered. She slowly loosened the string. I stepped away from the wall.

"You're a Rangerian," Bancroft said, echoing my words. "A True Born gone rogue. Am I wrong?" She didn't reply. "Who are you?" Bancroft gripped his sword tighter. "Why have you been following us?"

"Drop your bow," Nick ordered, stepping forward with his blade drawn. The archer's bow clattered to the stone.

Bancroft reached forward and jerked off her hood. A long, dark braid fell down her back. Her mismatched eyes were so dark they were almost black. Bancroft drew back, keeping his sword trained on her.

"My name is Niskian Fortunati." She looked up at me with those black eyes, and a chill ran down my spine. Her eyes shifted to Nick, "I am Rangerian of Shadow."

Daetho's warning yowl pierced the air. Shadows were appearing in the fog around us. Niskian suddenly darted out of Bancroft's hold. Her sword appeared in her black-gloved hand, a sword unlike anything I had seen, black tendrils of Shadow all swirling together to form the blade.

"Where is the Arrow?" she shouted. More and more figures appeared in the haze. She glanced over her shoulder. She snatched up her bow, swung it onto her back, then faded into nothing but a dark Shadow, lost in the swirling fog.

"It's a trap!" Bancroft cried. He pivoted, raising his sword.

I gripped my hilt tight. Ice-cold Wind blew past me. *They didn't have to chase me. I had caught up with them.*

"You're cornered, Jack." Orin Iversen stepped out of the fog with a smile. Daniel and the Sheriff followed behind him, the rest of the Hunters circling around us.

"You did good, boy." Sheriff Androuet clapped Orin on the back and pushed past him. Orin clenched his fists and a wall of hot Wind burst up in front of him. The Sheriff stopped.

"I'm not a boy," he growled. Androuet ignored him and stepped down off the rubble. Daniel stopped, folding his arms behind his back.

The Sheriff smiled through his anger and held out his arms. "Jackson! Good to meet you again."

I backed away, leveling my sword. Bancroft, Natanian, and Nick moved between him and me. The Hunters stopped. Sheriff Androuet's eyes flickered to Nick standing beside me, and a look that could not be mistaken for anything short of pure terror flashed across his face.

Orin grinned, "Come on, Jackson. *We'll make history.*"

"There's no way we can get out of this," Bancroft whispered to us. "Just get back to the Perytons. Whatever it takes. Understood?" *They were here for me. This was a trap. That message was probably sent long after Fort Calmier was destroyed.* More figures were appearing out of the mist, *every one of them Rangerians.*

Orin took another step forward, "Don't listen to him, Jackson."

"I'm not sure we will make it down to the Perytons, Bancroft," Daetho growled. Natanian raised his fingers to whistle for the steeds.

Bancroft slapped his hand away. *"Don't,"* he warned. "If you summon them here, they'll be shot down."

I glanced over my shoulder, searching desperately for an escape route.

"Bring him out!" Sheriff Androuet shouted over his shoulder. Two Hunters emerged from the fog, leading an Áccyn soldier.

I froze in place. My head reeled. *This shouldn't be possible.* The man's blond hair was tangled and dirty, his face jaundiced, a bandage wrapped tightly around his side beneath his leather armor.

"Master Kane!" I gasped. My first Master's blue eyes found me in the fog. I pushed past Bancroft and Nick to see clearly. *I saw him fall before Androuet, I thought he was dead...*

"Jack, this is a trap," he blurted out. "The Sorcerer did this. He's backing up the Hunters now."

One of the Hunters knocked Kane down to the stone. I lunged forward, but Bancroft caught my arm, holding me back. I heard the Sheriff shift, and saw his eyes dart to Nick with that same flash of fear. I glanced over my shoulder at my best friend. He was watching Daniel, anger flaring behind his eyes. Kane painfully pushed himself upright.

"How did you...?" I shook my head. The air hummed with energy from all the Rangerians around us. The very ground trembled.

"You have to run!" my first Master screamed. The Hunter clapped a hand around his throat, hissing something into his face. And Rangerian Fire exploded through the fog, a roaring Inferno flaring into the night sky.

Out of the fog stepped Karalie, Flames twisting up her arms, her braids tied back in a ponytail, rippling in the heat. My heart leapt.

"Jack, this way!" she shouted.

Ealdra Rangerians, whom I suddenly recognized as Áccyn in disguise, surged from the shadowed masses. Cold Wind whipped up around me.

"Grab him." Orin commanded, his smile gone. Hunters lurched forward.

"Jack!" Kara shouted.

I spun on my heel and tore after her across the courtyard and into the castle ruins.

THIRTY

I BURST THROUGH THE throne room door, Natanian, Nick, and Daetho piling in behind me. The Hunters were sprinting down the hall toward us. I slammed the door closed after us.

A jet of Water hit the door on the other side, sending a shudder through the wood. I jumped back, stepping up onto a council table beside Kara.

She flashed me a grin. "Welcome to the party."

I grabbed her arm, pulling her into a tight hug. My heart was hammering against my chest, relief washing over me. I shut my eyes tight, her arms warm around me.

With a squeeze, she let go, "Glad you're not dead, Jack."

"I'm sorry I left you behind..." All the words began spilling out, everything I couldn't say, should've said, and then didn't have a chance to say. "Kara, I know I should never have left you with Daniel. I should have gone back—"

"Shut up, Jack! We've got bad guys breaking down the door."

"Right." I swallowed, gripping my sword tight.

She reached down and squeezed my hand, flashing a smile. "I missed your stupid face too."

The door exploded with a resounding *crash* in a burst of Water.

"Got a plan, Kara?" Nick yelled.

"Nope, this was as far as I got."

"Oh, awesome," Natanian said sarcastically.

Daniel stepped through the remains of the door, the Hunters behind him. The back of the throne room was blown out, and two of the pillars had crashed to the ground. The ceiling above us creaked dangerously.

"Guys! Get out through there." I nodded to my left, to the side door which led out to the bell tower.

An Ealdra Rangerian stepped through the door after Daniel, and vines began twisting up the pillars, started to close around us, blocking the way out. Nick lunged and grabbed hold of the twisting vines. Lightning split through the wood.

Fire roared up around Kara. I jumped back. She glanced at us, her dark skin glowing in the Flames. I crouched on the table, gauging the distance between the Hunters and me. It was time to make a stand.

"I'm done running." My voice pounded through the throne room.

"I told you to *get him!*" Orin roared, the Sheriff and him shoving past Daniel.

The Hunters surged forward. I launched myself up off the table and raised my sword high above my head as ice-cold Wind twisted through the throne room, whipping Kara's Fire up around us. I swung my sword down as Sheriff Androuet threw up his blade. I landed on the stone and spun, twisting free of his parry.

He swung again. I jumped back and stabbed forward. My blade glanced off his armor and victory flickered behind his eyes.

The vines around us were now on fire. Cold energy tingled from my chest toward my fingers. I stepped back and slammed my hands together. Gray mist streamed down my sword. I spun my blade in my hand and lunged forward, swinging it up, knocking Androuet's blade away. I twisted, my sword clashing into his. Wind burst from my blade, and his sword flew from his hand, clattering to the stone. The victory turned to worry behind his eyes.

I growled, "You should have stayed in the shadows."

"Get down!" Daetho shouted.

From across the hall, a blast of Water left Daniel's hands. I dove. Fire roared up behind me and exploded against the blast, hot steam billowing through the throne room. Daniel's Water split, roaring dark, twisting around us. Androuet snatched his long sword off the stone.

A wall of Shadow shot up in front of us. The Water crashed to the ground, cracking the tile. The Dark Archer appeared in the doorway behind me.

"Come on!" she shouted.

"Who's that?" Kara looked around at me.

"Khadija!" Daetho shouted. Khadija swung up on his back and leaned flat against his neck.

"I've got them." Kara's eyes flared. Fire roared up her arms.

"Kara, no!" I shouted.

"*Jackson!*" the Dark Archer roared.

I grabbed Kara's arm and took off, the others right behind me. A shout rang from the ranks of soldiers, and they surged forward. The archer swept through the doorway. Energy and light flashed behind us as the Rangerians took their shots. An ear-splitting clap of thunder echoed off the stone.

The side hallway was gone, only the steps leading up to the bell tower hanging blackened and half-broken ahead. Niskian—the Dark Archer—spun around and threw up her hands. The two pillars closest to the door were hit with a blast of Shadow and crashed into the doorway. I threw up my arms, shielding my head as rubble rained down around us.

Slowly I stood up, coughing in the cloud of dust. Shouts echoed from inside. It sounded like the entire castle was creaking and groaning, beginning to collapse. We had to get out of here.

"Thanks," I coughed, giving a thumbs-up to the Dark Archer.

"You're no good to me captured."

"I don't think they were aiming to capture us," I pointed out.

"Do you *want* to die, Descendant of Rowan?" she snapped.

Kara stepped forward. "Excuse me, who are you?"

"Wait a minute... *where's Nick?*" I shouted. He was right behind me. Now I couldn't even hear his Thunder.

"Oh, no." Bancroft stared back at the rubble-filled doorway. He took off, sprinting back around to find another way in. *"Nicolas!"*

"Get to the Perytons!" Daetho shouted.

We heeded his command, scrambling up the creaking steps toward the bell tower. I took one last look back at the collapsed stone, hoping against hope that Nick would burst through. Fire flared beneath Kara's hands as she touched the wood of the railing, leaving scorch marks behind her.

"Hey, stop leaving breadcrumbs," I chided. "We *don't* want them to follow us, Kara!"

"Shut up, Jack!"

I shot her a smirk.

I climbed up the last step as the others ahead of me turned onto the battlements and faded into the fog. The wood beneath my feet was blackened, scattered with debris. I glanced up at the bell on the level above me. It hung still, dead silent to the siege around it. I stepped off the wooden walkway and onto the stone of the battlements, running after my friends.

It felt like a truck slammed into me. I went airborne, flying through the fog. I flailed for the edge of the walkway and grabbed hold at the last second. I slammed back into the tower and the air was shoved from my lungs. I wheezed for breath, glancing down. *Forty feet to the courtyard floor.*

I tossed my sword up onto the walkway and grabbed hold with my other hand, scrambling up. Pain shot through my injured leg.

Out of the darkness before me, Orin appeared, the fog swirling around him in a tornado, suspending him in the air. "You can't get away that easily," he snarled.

Someone grabbed my arm, and the space plunged into darkness. Dim shapes shifted before me, the world in shades of gray.

Orin dropped onto the walkway. *"Jackson!"* he shouted, "You can't hide forever!" I twisted around to see Niskian standing beside me, her hand closed around my arm.

I snatched up my sword, "What's going on?"

"*Shh,*" she ordered, her grip like iron around my arm.

"Let me go!" She started running, pulling me after her, right past Orin, racing up the tower steps to the bell. "We're... we're *invisible,*" I stammered.

"Only if you keep quiet," she hissed.

"How is this possible? How can you—"

"There's no time. Now keep quiet, or they *will* find us."

Below us, Orin shouted in frustration and leaped off the walkway. His Wind caught him and he drifted down, soaring back toward the main courtyard.

Niskian suddenly let go and turned on me, slamming the hilt of her sword into my injured thigh. Tendrils of Shadow snaked into the wound. The world shot back into color and light. I gasped through my teeth and staggered away, collapsing back against the rail as hot pain stabbed through my leg. I pressed my hand to my thigh. Blood seeped through the bandages.

Niskian raised her sword. "Now answer me! *Where is the Golden Arrow?*"

THIRTY-ONE

I STOOD ALONE ON the top of the bell tower, my friends gone, thick fog swirling around me, staring straight into the flashing black eyes of the Dark Archer.

She trained her sword on me. *"Where is the Golden Arrow?"* she repeated.

I clenched my teeth against the throbbing pain in my leg and tightened my grip on my sword. "How am I supposed to know?"

"I know Rowan Tyler found it. W*here is it?"*

"I still don't know what you're talking about."

She lunged forward. I dove aside, swinging my blade up. She whipped around and caught it, throwing me backward. She raised her hand, and dark Smoke curled up her arm. Her Shadow twisting through my injured leg stabbed sharply, and I lost my balance and fell back against the rail. My head reeled.

"Stop lying to me."

"Why have you been following us?"

"Because you *know where it is!*" A blast of dark energy shot from her hand.

I spun away. Wind whipped around me, swinging the bell. A *clang* echoed through the air. I glanced down at my hand, red from my own blood.

Niskian lunged, shoving me back into the railing. *"Do you have any idea what stakes are riding on this?"* she hissed.

"How could I possibly know where a thousand-year-old stick of gold is?" My voice cracked in a fresh wave of pain.

She leaned into me, her face inches from mine. *"There are things going on you have no idea about, dear Jackson."* Her breath rushed past my ear, hot in the cold air. "Why do you think the Ealdra seized Fort Calmier? Why do you think they're hunting you? *How do you think the Ealdra were able to get in, in the first place?*" She grabbed my arm. "There's a spy, Jackson. A spy who's been feeding the Ealdra and the Sheriff everything about you and the Áccyn. He's so much more dangerous than you could imagine... *and he's been right in front of you!"*

I pushed her away, lightheaded from the pain. "I know about the spy!" I pulled away from her and limped around the bell, putting some distance between us, raising my sword. Cold Wind whipped the fog around me into a small tornado.

She ducked under the bell. "The Ealdra found a weapon, Jackson. But to get it, they need *you*. They need *your* power. That's why you're being hunted."

"You really need to rethink your information sources. I know all this. Everyone does. Common knowledge, *dear archer."* I shrugged, my heart pounding in my chest. As I backed away from her, her Shadow pierced my injury again. I muffled my grunt of pain.

"Once they find out what this Golden Arrow can *really* do," she whispered, "they're going after it too. They're planning a *war*. After almost a thousand years, they're mounting their power, they're about to wipe out the Áccyn and *everyone else."* She raised her dark blade, Shadow twisting around it. I stopped, cornered against the railing. "So, I need you to tell me where your sweet grandpa hid the Arrow. *Because you're right in the middle of this, and you don't want me as your enemy.*"

In the courtyard below, Rangerians appeared in the fog. I tightened my grip on my sword and took a deep breath, letting the pain drift away.

There was no one to get me out of this one.

I was going to have to fight my way out.

Niskian strode toward me, her hood fallen, her long braid tossed behind her. Her sword twisted with darkness. She suddenly lunged, stepped up onto the rail, and leaped toward me, falling through the air.

I dropped and whirled away, bringing my sword around in a wide arc. Niskian ducked away from my cut. I sprang to my feet, slashing again. She threw up her blade. The metal hit with a resounding clash. I saw the dark Smoke forming in her hand. I spun aside. It shot past my head and exploded against the bell, sending another ringing toll through the ruins. I dove forward, caught her sword, and kicked out. She staggered back.

I summoned all of my power and screamed, letting all the anger and terror and pain rush out. A monstrous blast of cold Wind jetted out from me. Niskian flew backward, hit one of the support posts, and slammed into the floor. She lay, dazed. The Shadow seeped from my wound and vanished into fog, and my pain with it.

I grabbed hold of the rail and swung over, dropping the eight feet through the air. I landed back on the castle walls, my injured thigh slamming against the stone battlements. If only I could make it to Perry...

Niskian fell towards me. She hit the wall behind me and spun, the hilt of her sword smashing into my shoulder. I slammed into the battlement wall again and bounced off. I scrambled back, and rolled my shoulder in its socket with a grimace. It felt bruised from her strike. Very bruised. She swung. I jumped back and stabbed. She caught my blade and threw me off again.

The air was buzzing with Rangerian energy. I had lost sight of the others long ago. I could only hope they were still safe. "You used to be Áccyn, right?" I called.

She laughed. "You should listen to me. Tell me where it is."

I backed away around the corner and down the walkway. "I told you, I don't know." Most of the roof was gone and several pillars had toppled in the middle of the path. The walkway itself stopped halfway to the other side of the courtyard. The rest of it lay in pieces on the stone below.

I stopped in my tracks. There went that plan. I could see the hall I needed to get to twenty feet on the other side of the gap. That hall was the only way down to Perry. I frantically glanced around for another way, my stomach twisting.

Niskian advanced, raised her sword, and struck. I spun around and threw up my blade, knocking hers away. It bounced off the stone.

She swung again. I knocked it away. Again her sword rang off a column. She lunged forward and slashed. I sidestepped, spinning to face her. My foot caught the edge of the walkway, and I slipped. I grabbed a column, steadying myself. *Not again. I can't fall again.*

"I warned you." Her eyes flashed dark. She threw her arms forward with a shout, hurling all her might into her power. A dark jet blasted from her hands and slammed into my chest. I flew back through the air.

I saw the floor drop out from beneath me.

My heart stopped. I threw out my arms and caught hold of the edge of the walkway. My shoulder, bruised from her strike, screamed in pain. It had to be fractured, at the very least. The stone began to crumble beneath my hands. My sword clattered to the stone forty feet below. My heart was racing against my ribs.

With what was left of my strength, I threw my arm over the top, took a breath, and started to pull myself up, straining against the pain. More stone crumbled beneath my hands.

The Dark Archer appeared above me. Her Shadow blade disappeared into smoke as unslung her bow and notched an arrow, drawing the string back. "Fine," she growled. "Don't tell me."

I saw the shining tip, the sharp edges glinting.

The black feathers rippled in the wind.

Her eyes narrowed, filled with rage.

I could smell the air burning with energy, feel the rough stone against my arms. Her leather boots creaked as she braced her foot on the stone. The wind blew back the loose strands of her braid. The stone shifted beneath my hands.

She let out her breath.

The stone gave out under me.

Thirty-Two

THE DARK ARCHER'S ARROW whistled past, the black fletching brushing the top of my head. I was falling through the air, fog swirling up around me.

Then I slammed into something, and I felt it push me upward. I was flying through the air, circling low. The world came back into focus. Perry twisted around, blinking at me with one shining eye. I couldn't move, frozen in shock, my heart still racing from the fall. An Ealdra archer below raised his bow. Perry banked sideways. The arrow sailed by. Perry turned upward and accelerated, rising high above the castle and the fog.

I shook the shock off. From my perch, I saw Nick battling Daniel, Lightning flashing through his Water across the ruins. Natanian and Bancroft were backing slowly, standing between the stables and the oncoming ranks of Rangerians. I couldn't find Kara in the chaos.

There was someone else standing there in the fog. A dark shadow that had just appeared. I glanced back over my shoulder. Niskian stood at the edge of the walkway, watching me fly away. A shiver ran down my spine. The person in the courtyard below me was not the Dark Archer.

Whoever it was raised her hands and blasted the fog away, leaving only curling tendrils on the stone at her feet. The Áccyn forces were being repelled by the Ealdra Rangerians. Behind the woman, the Sheriff stood guarding my Master Kane.

I swallowed the bad taste in my mouth. "Perry, down!" We dove for the courtyard. The woman turned around. A towering, red crown rose on her head.

"No, Jackson, get out of here!" Bancroft shouted, waving at me.

The Red Queen looked around at the Áccyn soldiers and smiled, an expression that sent cold shooting out through my veins, one in which I saw a thousand lives lost.

I landed in what had once been the training arena and slid off Perry. One by one, Daniel and the rest of the Ealdra Rangerians dropped to their knees, bowing their heads. The Áccyn soldiers edged away, watching nervously. Nick lowered his sword, falling back beside Bancroft. He brushed his hair out of his eyes, staring at the Red Queen. Kara burst from the Áccyn ranks and skidded to a stop. Her sandy hair was blackened with soot.

Now what? I looked around, my heart pounding. I saw my sword lying a good fifteen feet beneath the walkway, with three Ealdra Rangerians between me and the weapon. Above me, Niskian was silently watching, sizing up the lady. Then she pulled up her hood and faded into Shadow. Nick's eyes trailed after her.

"Awesome," I muttered to myself. *If the Dark Archer was afraid of this woman...*

I sidled around to the others, "Who's that?"

"The Ealdra queen," Daetho murmured, stepping from the ranks with Khadija and Colton.

"What's she doing here?" I whispered.

Her eyes found mine. "Hi, Jack." She began moving toward me, seeming to glide above the stone. "I can feel the power inside you."

My fingers felt cold. Wind whispered across my arms, chilling my skin.

Thick vines burst from the stone, tangling around the others' legs, dragging them back. Fire flared around Kara, searing through the vines, but more of them twisted around her, more tightly. Ice curled in sharp patterns over the wood as Natanian struggled. I saw the Rangerian responsible standing behind the Hunters, thin vines twisting up through his long, red hair.

"Jackson, leave us!" Daetho shouted. *"Run!"*

"No!" My voice tore at my throat, my fists clenched around my roaring Wind.

The queen raised her hand, and a wall of darkness burst up between us, throwing me off my feet. It shot around the courtyard, twisting black. We were enveloped in the eye of the storm. I regained my balance. The queen, the Sheriff, and Orin stood a few feet away. I was alone with them, cut off from any help, all outside sounds muffled. My sword was gone.

Thick vines shot from under the wall of darkness and lashed around my legs, pulling me to the stone. My hands hit the ground. The branches cut into my injured thigh. I screamed in pain and fear, jerking against the vines. They snaked up around my body, twisting around my arms and chest. My Wind whipped around me, churning the wall of darkness in twisting tendrils, spiraling up all around us.

The Red Queen crouched down in front of me, my Wind rippling through her hair. She raised her hand toward me, her thin lips split in a smile, the reflected light off her crowning shining on her high cheekbones, dark eyebrows, her wide eyes. I struggled with all my might against the vines tightening around me.

"You're so cute," she whispered. Her fingers brushed my face, trailing down my throat, pressing into my chest, reaching for my power. "You're just a tiny baby. But you're so strong. Can you feel it? Inside you?"

My muscles tensed, straining desperately. "Let me go," I croaked. The wall of darkness behind me seemed to suck up all light and sound. It was sorcery as I had never seen before.

So strong, she repeated. "How long has it been, Jack? How long have you had this power? Not long, right? Not long enough to control it."

She stood up. My swirling Wind pooled in her palm. I struggled with all my might, straining against the vines that lashed me to the stone. *It was all done. It was all about to end here. All these days of running and fighting for my life, it was all about to end.* My eyes moved past her to Androuet and Orin.

"You were so scared of the little Sheriff." Her words echoed hauntingly in the vortex around us. "But didn't you realize what was going to happen when he brought you to the one who commissioned him?"

I couldn't breathe, the cold air straining through my throat, the vines tightening around my chest, around my injured shoulder, squeezing into the pain. *I was going to die here.*

A familiar voice shouted in anger. Two Hunters brought Khadija, struggling, through the wall of darkness. They forced her down in front of me. Vines lashed up around her arms and legs. She strained, gasping.

The queen stepped back as Orin moved around us. I heard him draw his sword. He bent forward, touching the tip to Khadija's neck. She froze, shaking, and my Wind twisted up in a swirling tornado around us.

"Welcome, Princess Krom." Orin tilted his head. "Or, should I say... *former* princess. You deserted your court, didn't you?"

The final Wind Rangerian—Dillon—was brought through the wall of darkness and shoved down beside me. He looked beaten. *The boy who had disappeared only a few days before my Manifestation...* I knew him. Recognized him from Fort Calmier. I think he served guard duty the shift after me. He lived a few floors up from my room.

"Good work, Orin." Sheriff Androuet flashed him a degrading look as he moved forward. "Now let's finish the job, *my queen.*" He nodded to the lady.

"*Androuet!*" Orin shouted, rage flashing across his face.

The queen shot them a dangerous glance. They backed away from each other.

Orin sheathed his sword, strode forward, and seized hold of the vines twisting around my wrist. More vines curled around Khadija's wrists. He grabbed hold, wrapping them around his own, so his fingers brushed mine.

"*Khadija,*" I whispered. She looked up, her eyes wide in terror. Her chest was heaving. Sparks of ice and fire flickered around her. I nodded as if to say, *It's going to be okay.*

The Sheriff lashed Dillon to the rest of us.

We knelt on the cold stone of the courtyard, the sorcerer queen's wall of darkness twisting around us, bound in a circle by dark vines. I strained against my bonds as they tightened around me, pain aching in my shoulder and leg. The queen moved forward, reached into the folds of her robe, and pulled out an old, torn piece of paper. I took a shallow, shaky breath.

She smiled at us, her thin lips drawing back from her teeth, and began to read, words I couldn't make out rolling beneath her breath. Fog seeped from her robes, pooling at her feet. *I couldn't get free. I couldn't get out. I didn't know if we were going to make it out alive... or if I had just lied to Khadija. Maybe it wasn't going to be okay...*

The cold in my chest began to press painfully hard against my ribs. *We were going to die here.* I could feel Dillon straining against his bonds. Orin clenched his fists tight. The pain in my chest grew worse. I gritted my teeth and shut my eyes. Wind whistled in my ears. It felt like something was in my chest, pounding against my ribs with a stone.

I cried out. A pulse of cold Wind burst from me. My eyes flew open. Wind was twisting up around us, occasional flickers of fire and ice shooting up the twirling cyclone. The queen's voice rose, and she took a step closer to us.

The pain in my chest faltered a moment, then renewed again, twice as strong. My head fell to my chest and I groaned through my teeth. I strained against the vines holding me in place. The Wind, the energy, pulsed from the four of us in rings, rippling through the haze.

Then I felt another energy. One that was hot, powerful, sucking in everything around it. I slowly raised my head, straining against the pain. A brilliant, golden light ricocheted in the space between us. A shape shifted in the center of the light, wisps of our Wind being sucked together to form a human figure. The pain stabbed into my chest, and I doubled over with a cry.

My power was being ripped from my body. I couldn't let that happen. *I was just beginning to find control.*

I couldn't run anymore. No one and nothing was going to save me. Not any Master, not my great-grandfather's legacy, not the Áccyn. My sword was gone. Fort Calmier was destroyed. My friends were being held captive. The Ealdra did not care if I lived or died.

But I had escaped from the Ealdra palace. I had escaped from the Dark Archer. *I had to escape from this.*

The golden light between us grew brighter. Khadija's unrestrained power was sending sparks of energy shooting into the tornado around us. The Ealdra queen raised her hands, and the golden light flared. Searing pain stabbed my chest. My heart was being torn from its cage.

I threw my head back and screamed. My power burst free in a tremendous blast. The vines binding me shattered. I fell onto my hands. The whirling cyclone dropped. The wall of darkness flickered. The golden light glowed alone in the darkness.

"No!" Orin screamed. He was on his knees, his face ashen-white. He grabbed at my wrist, trying to connect us again. I gritted my teeth and slammed my palm into the stone. A shockwave blasted out, throwing the

Ealdra queen, the Hunters, Orin, Khadija, and Dillon flat on their backs.

The wall of darkness shattered. The golden light flickered and vanished. The figure who was inside staggered, falling to one knee.

I pushed myself to my feet, breathing hard. Gray mist twisted down my arms. Ice-cold Wind whipped up the thick fog in a swirling tornado around me. I bent down and picked up Orin's fallen sword, turning to face the figure before me.

It was a man. He slowly stood up. His dark brown hair fell around his face. He held out his arms, looking them up and down. Dull brown robes draped off his shoulders. His head came up, and his eyes fixed on mine. Gold light pulsed behind his eyes, then faded out to an eerie yellow-green.

The Ealdra queen removed her crown and knelt before him. "My King." He turned to face her. I gripped Orin's sword tight, and took a step forward. Pain stabbed my chest. I stopped with a gasp, pressing my hand over my heart. I was half-relieved to find I did in fact still possess a heart, the pulse beating against my palm. I straightened. The Ealdra queen stood and held out her arm, "Come with me, My King." He held up his hand, silencing her. He took a step toward me and tilted his head, watching at me with curiosity.

I raised Orin's sword and took a step forward. "Leave," I ordered. "Before I show you who I am." My voice shook. Gray fog twisted down my blade. I felt a power rising in me as I had never felt, not in all my fear and pain.

The king held out his hand. The queen rested her hand on his arm, and they vanished in a swirl of fog.

I heard a rustle behind me. As Orin pushed himself to his feet, I turned to face him, raising my sword. Ealdra soldiers ran past me, out of the ruins, out of Fort Calmier. It was done.

"What are you *doing?*" Orin screamed, his eyes flashing in rage. He clenched his fists, and fog twisted up his arms. I could feel the heat radiating from him, but something was wrong. It was like his power kept shorting out. The Golden King had sapped his strength. I took a step forward. The swirling tornado around me held strong.

Behind him, my friends staggered to their feet. Orin threw his hands forward with a scream of fury. I raised my arm, and our blasts of Wind slammed into each other, bursting in a ringing *boom*. The tornado twisted faster around me, and my feet left the ground. I raised my arms, balancing myself as I levitated off the stone. Orin shot into the air, rising up to meet me. Then his power failed, and he dropped to the ground. He scrambled to his feet, drawing his long dagger. I raised my hand, and his knife flew from his grip.

Nick, now free, grabbed hold of Orin's armor and shoved him to his knees. Natanian and Kara moved forward, pinning Orin down. I lowered my arms, drifting back to the ground. I landed on the stone and stumbled a step. I lowered my sword, the Wind dying away. Colton sprinted past me toward Khadija. Master Kane staggered forward and threw his arms around me, pulling me into a weak hug. He stepped back and clapped a hand on my shoulder. A *boom* of thunder crashed through the air.

I spun to look at Nick. He staggered back. Orin trembled with the force of the shock. Nick collapsed to his knees, Sparks shooting out across his shoulders.

"Are you okay?" I asked him.

"I'm fine," he snapped. He inhaled sharply and pressed his palm to his forehead. He forced himself to his feet, lowering his hand. He took a deep, shaking breath.

"We need to get away from here," Daetho said. "Far away." His eyes met mine. I nodded. "We need to get to Lake Cloudia."

THIRTY-THREE

"**A**RE YOU SURE YOU can't come with us?" I sighed, looking up at my parents. Áccyn soldiers moved around us, setting up camp in the woods, miles away from Fort Calmier.

My dad gestured around us. "We need to help rebuild." Most of the makeshift tents were up. Some campfires had been lit, over which the remaining Áccyn soldiers cooked food. Carts of weapons and supplies rolled past. Soldiers grabbed what they needed, returning to their tents beneath the trees of the forest. Fort Calmier was gone. But the people remained.

"Your place is with your friends," my dad said. "The Azomien will protect you. This is not even the beginning of what the Ealdra are capable of."

I threw my arms around my dad, hugging him tight. My mom wrapped us both in an embrace.

"You are stronger than you know, Jack," she whispered.

"Jackson." Daetho paced up to me, his fur singed from battle. I waved goodbye to my parents and followed him through the trees to where my friends stood waiting beside their Perytons.

I swung up on Perry and took one last look back at my court, at the makeshift tents and the torches strung through the woods. Then I leaned forward and patted Perry's neck, "Come on, boy. Let's go."

I slid off Perry, onto the gray pebbles that spread across the shoreline. We were on an island in the middle of a deep, blue lake. Twisting trees and vines rose before me, tangling together. The others swung off their Perytons behind me.

"This way." Daetho followed a path cut through the jungle of trees. Smooth gray stones lined the way. I rubbed Perry's back as we walked. He turned to look at me, a clump of tasty vines he'd found hanging from his mouth.

I laughed, "Good boy."

"Stay here," Daetho called. We drew to a stop, and he moved forward, disappearing through a tangle of hanging vines.

I shifted nervously, bracing my hand on Orin's sword in my sheath. Orin himself stood silently behind me, his bonds held tight by Natanian. Bancroft moved up beside me.

"Have you been here before?" I whispered.

"No," Bancroft answered. "Not many have. The Azomien are very secretive. They don't like visitors."

Daetho emerged from the vines. "You may follow me."

I swallowed, and stepped forward, pushing aside the vines. A towering tree rose so high into the air I could not see its crest, the smooth, dark bark twisting in patterns up into its leaves. The branches fanned out farther than I could see, hanging with thick vines. Small lights flickered up the trunk. Water curled through and around the roots in small streams, cascading down into a series of pools.

Thin rays of sunlight streamed through the branches above. A flock of blue birds soared around the lower branches and disappeared into the jungle. The wide, flat, gray stones of the pools were woven with veins of lichen and moss. At the foot of the tree, the roots separated to reveal a small opening hidden behind vines.

The others stepped through behind me. Panthers speckled with gold, just like Daetho, were sitting or standing on the rocks leading up to the opening in the tree.

"Welcome to Lake Cloudia." Daetho turned to look back at Khadija and me. "Here you will be safe from the Ealdra, from the Sorcerer. The defenses put up were made just for his power."

"Welcome, Great Guardian of the North," another Azomien bowed his head.

"Thanks. Nice place." I nodded, my stomach doing a flip. My grandpa must have come here before. This is where he must have gotten that name... the name that was now mine.

THIRTY-FOUR

I SAT ON A large stone, dangling my feet in the pool beneath me. A cooling cream soothed the gash on my leg, and my bruised shoulder was bandaged tight. I could barely feel the pain now. Daetho was in council with several of the other Azomien, in the small room at the base of the tree. The rest of the cats were taking an evening nap.

The stone was cool beneath me, the sound of the trickling waterfalls refreshing. My satchel sat on the rock beside me. I riffled through the pictures in my hands.

Grandpa Tyler had been to Lake Cloudia too. Maybe they had brought him here to train. *One day, Jack*, he used to say, *One day you, too, will become a guardian. One day, I know you will find your own band of merry men all!*

I laughed to myself. I *did* find my own band of 'merry men all!' I had Nick, Natanian, Kara, Bancroft, Kane... descendants of Robin Hood, *soldiers.*

Natanian sat down next to me. "How'd it go with the cats?" I started. He laughed. "I interrupted a thought, didn't I? Well, what was it?"

"I was just thinking about my grandpa again."

"Is that him?" Kara sat down on my other side and tugged the stack of photos from me. I leaned back on my elbow. She held one up, grinning.

"What?"

She squinted. "You look nothing alike." I grabbed for them. Kara laughed and handed the photos back to me, stretching out on the bank of the pool.

Nick sat down next to us. "What's so funny?"

"Jack's grandpa," Natanian answered.

Nick grinned, "Oh, yeah."

I shoved the photos back into the satchel and shook my head.

"So, Nick," I started, changing the subject, "I've been meaning to ask you something."

He swung one leg up on the stone. "Shoot."

"What's the deal with you and Daniel?"

Natanian sat up. "Yeah, what *is* the deal? Why, out of *all* the Ealdra soldiers, does *Daniel,* in particular, want to kill you?"

"You met him again before last night, didn't you?" Kara looked up.

Nick grimaced. "It's... a long story."

I shrugged. "What else do we have to do right now?"

"I'm free all afternoon." Kara folded her arms behind her head, sending him a mischievous smirk.

Nick sighed. "Fine." He paused. "For starters, Daniel and I grew up together in the Ealdra court. But I was the crown prince, and he was the son of a guard. As we grew older, he got jealous. I had special training."

"Wait, *what?*" Kara sat up. "Crown prince?" Natanian and I laughed.

"At your service." Nick smiled.

"But..." She laid back down, still confused.

"A few times, I caught Daniel sneaking out of the castle to practice by himself," Nick continued. "When our powers manifested, he grew angry because I had all the highest Masters. He had to work five times harder to even *begin* to learn control. He had already begun to hate me. But he was strong and growing stronger. In fact, he was well on his way to surpassing me, he had such drive." Nick dropped his head.

"I heard the courtiers whispering about the possibility of him being second in line for the throne—as *my* successor. Until I had an heir, that position was up for—" Nick let out a faint grunt of pain and pressed his hand to his forehead.

Kara sat up.

I frowned. "What's wrong?"

He shook his head, "Nothing. It's just a headache."

"So, what happened?" Natanian pushed.

Nick breathed out, and lowered his hand. "Daniel's father was on duty the night I ran away. I couldn't control my power very well, and... he got in the way. It wasn't my fault. *They shouldn't have tried to stop me.*" His hand clenched around the moss on the stone, his knuckles turning white. "Then we went back to the castle. *And they sent Daniel. They shouldn't have drawn so much attention. I told them not to send someone th—*" Nick stopped suddenly at the look on my face. I glanced at Natanian, a terrible crawling feeling sinking into my stomach. "...someone that dangerous," Nick finished slowly.

But the damage was done. My head was buzzing, spinning. *No, no, no,* a small voice was screaming into my head.

There's no other way the Ealdra could have known about us, Bancroft had said.

"What did you say?" I whispered, sitting up, staring into the water, my hands clenched tight on the edge of the rock, my heart pounding. I felt ice-cold. And I didn't think it was my Wind. I was hoping upon hope that I had heard wrong. Maybe the healing medicine the Azomien gave me was fogging my mind.

Nick gave a soft laugh. "I said, I told them not to send someone that dangerous." The water below us rippled with a pulse of my Wind. Natanian stood up. Kara looked around, confused.

Information of our every move. Being sent back to the Ealdra... the attack on Fort Calmier... the Sheriff and Hunters in the forest... the army waiting in the ruins... Daniel.

"Nick." I looked up. "Did we end up in that forest on purpose?"

Nick stared at me, the color beginning to fade from his cheeks. Lightning crackled up his arms, his hand pressing into the stone. Then he slammed his hand into the side of his head.

I stood up. *No, no, no, no*, the voice was screaming in the back of my head. My fingers closed around my sword hilt as Kara rose to her feet. My hands were shaking.

"You're *the Ealdra spy*." My voice was hoarse. *"Nick..."*

"You," he looked up at me, grinning. There was something *there* behind his eyes, a flicker of green light, something I didn't recognize. "You were the fourth Wind. You were the one thing we needed to finish."

He stood up. "I wasn't sure though. I wasn't sure until it manifested. Then I realized you were *much* more than just another Wind Rangerian. Your power was the strongest anyone had ever seen." He shook his head. "The Hunters couldn't be trusted to take you in. *Androuet? Seriously?"* Nick barked a laugh. "Pathetic."

The Hunters... the look of fear on the Sheriff's face when he looked at Nick in Fort Calmier....

"Stop," Nick ordered. I frowned. He wasn't talking to us. He doubled over with a grunt.

I drew my sword. *"You* led the Ealdra and the Hunters to Fort Calmier. You're the one—"

Suddenly the *something* behind his eyes vanished and Nick cried out, "He's got ahold of me. *He's* the Sorcerer! I tried to stop—" Then he spun around with a curse and slammed his hand into his head again.

Natanian, Kara, and I froze, staring at him. I couldn't move. Blood rushed through my head. *The Dark Archer's warning, the way the Ealdra moved around him... avoiding him in terror.* Cold Wind rose around me. I braced myself, my throat dry. *Please.*

Then Nick straightened up, rolled his neck, and started laughing, his voice shattering the calm. *A flicker of green light behind his eyes.* Thick, cold fog curled around his feet, beginning to stream off his shoulders.

Finally, he shrugged. "Well, there it is."

"Where's Nick?" I screamed.

He took a step forward. "Oh, Jackson, Nick's been gone for years."

"How's that possible?" Kara demanded.

He tilted his head. "Didn't you hear what Nick said?" He pointed to his head. *"The Sorcerer,* Jackson."

"Daetho!" Natanian shouted for help.

Nick spun around and threw his arm out. Natanian and Kara threw up their hands. A jet of Lightning slammed into Natanian's wall of Ice and exploded, hurling them backward. Natanian slammed into the side of a tree and fell. Kara plunged into the pond, limp.

Nick threw up his hand, and an invisible force shoved my blade aside. *What was I doing? I couldn't kill him.* Fog swirled thick around our feet, spilling over the stones in the pools below. I raised my sword, staring at my *best friend.*

"Oh, I tried so hard, Jackson." He moved forward. I scrambled back. My foot hit the edge of the stone, and I froze. "I gave the Sheriff *so many* opportunities to catch up with you, and *every one of them failed.*"

I leveled my sword, gasping. He raised his hand, and my blade began to disintegrate into ashes, cracks racing down the metal toward my hands. I dropped it. It hit the stone with a resounding *clang* and dropped into the pool next to Kara in a hiss of steam.

The Azomien woke up and began to leap down from their perches on the trees.

"You're hurt, aren't you?" Nick's eyes drifted over my bandages, and searing pain stabbed into my shoulder, my leg. I screamed, falling forward. It felt as if a white-hot poker was being pressed into my injuries. I grabbed my shoulder. Nick crouched down in front of me, *"You don't belong here, Jackson."* The pain began to ebb, then a fresh wave crashed over me. I cried out.

"Nicolas!" I heard Bancroft shout. I collapsed, curling up. Bright spots burst in front of my eyes.

"Listen to me!" Nick demanded. He raised his hands. A shockwave shot out from him, sending the Azomien sliding to a stop. "Look at your defenses. So prepared for a grand attack you didn't even realize an *Ealdra* boy could slide through." He gestured at himself. *"I* created all this, *I* can bring it all crashing down!" His hand closed around my arm. As he yanked me to my feet, Natanian stirred. "What side are you on, Azomien? It is time to choose. A new power is rising, and it will sweep away all resistance."

Daetho let out a roar and leaped. Nick let go. I collapsed. Daetho slammed into him, hurling him back into the stone. Nick grinned, and melted into fog.

Daetho stared down at the fog as it faded away. Then he stepped back and turned to face the other Azomien, his eyes wide. "Alert the Áccyn. Throw up all our defenses around the Golden Arrow. Gisborne has a new host. The Ealdra are coming, and they will not be stopped."

I pressed my hand to my chest, stretching out my limbs. I felt the energy in my chest roar up.

Gasping, I breathed out the pain, and pushed myself off the ground.

ABOUT THE AUTHOR

Maggie K. West is an adventurer, researcher-of-many-things, and author. She is based in the Rocky Mountains, where there are forests, so obviously she's qualified to write a Robin Hood retelling. When she is not reading other people's novels, she plays D&D, goes on adventures with her dog Bilbo, and generally geeks out about things.

Stay up to date with all her shenanigans, and be the first to know about upcoming releases by joining her newsletter at www.maggiekwest.com/newsletter.

www.maggiekwest.com